FILTHY RICH TEMPTATION

RACHAEL STEWART

Boldwood

First published in Great Britain in 2025 by Boldwood Books Ltd.

Copyright © Rachael Stewart, 2025

Cover Design by Lori Jackson

Cover Images: Deposit Photos and Shutterstock

A CIP catalogue record for this book is available from the British Library.

Paperback ISBN 978-1-83633-183-4

Large Print ISBN 978-1-83633-182-7

Hardback ISBN 978-1-83633-181-0

Trade Paperback ISBN 978-1-80656-015-8

Ebook ISBN 978-1-83633-184-1

Kindle ISBN 978-1-83633-185-8

Audio CD ISBN 978-1-83633-176-6

MP3 CD ISBN 978-1-83633-177-3

Digital audio download ISBN 978-1-83633-180-3

This book is printed on certified sustainable paper. Boldwood Books is dedicated to putting sustainability at the heart of our business. For more information please visit https://www.boldwoodbooks.com/about-us/sustainability/

Boldwood Books Ltd, 23 Bowerdean Street, London, SW6 3TN

www.boldwoodbooks.com

For Parker, my little nephew and the spark behind Lottie. One day you'll be old enough to read this, until then, your parents can share the PG highlights ;-) Love you, monkey!
Aunty Rachael xxx

1

THEO

Something wakes me.

I'm not sure what.

I'm not sure I *want* to know.

It's early. Too early. The kind of early only birds and bakers should see.

But now I've heard it, I can't ignore it.

I roll onto my back and drag a hand down my face. How in the hell did it get to this? My life slowly being taken over by my best friend's little sister, Sadie, and her hurricane of a three-year-old, Lottie.

One week. That's all it's been since they moved in. One!

And sure, I said they could stay for the summer. Long enough for Sadie to find her feet, get sorted, and move on. But now?

Now I'm not sure who's going to surrender first – me, or them.

That's if the tenants downstairs don't file a noise complaint and force the issue first.

And I'm usually good at making decisions, sticking to them. But this one? This might be the one that breaks with tradition and breaks me in the process.

I stumble out of bed. Boxers. No shirt. Hair and glasses completely askew.

Dignity?

What's that again?

All I want is coffee. Maybe survival after that.

I like my life neat. Orderly. Predictable.

The exact opposite of the scene I find unfolding in my open-plan living space.

I adjust my specs and squint against the sunrise spilling through the floor-to-ceiling windows. Out there, London's skyline is bathed in gold, the Thames glinting like something out of a film. Calm. Cinematic.

In here? Toddler-powered carnage. And a noise that keeps on giving: squeals, huffs, a ding-a-ling-ding from God knows what. Though I can't see a soul – or a devil. Where on earth...?

I rake the hair from my eyes and pick my way through a graveyard of stuffed animals and plastic ponies, ignoring whatever's been smeared on the wood in between and—

'Shit!' A plastic truck spears my foot.

'OhmiGod!'

Sadie's head pops above the sofa, her blonde hair wild, her blue eyes wide as they lock onto mine. One second. Two. Then they shift south...

Naked chest.

Boxers.

Legs.

Boxers.

Boxers.

Boxers.

Her mouth parts in a soft, stunned *oh*, and every exhausted cell in my body sits up and pays attention. A memory from seven years ago launches into the present. Those lips. My mouth. Her tongue. My—

Double shit.

Clothes, next time. Clothes!

I make a break for the kitchen, needing to put a counter between her and my misbehaving body stat, when a tiny, pink trainer sails past my face. It smacks the wall with a soft thud and lands in my untouched fern like a sad little flag of surrender.

My youngest new roomie appears alongside her mother in a riot of blonde curls, her suspiciously sticky hands shooting into the air as she lets out a victorious squeal.

'I'm so sorry,' Sadie says, clambering to her feet and hefting a nappy sack the size of an unexploded bomb into view. 'She's still adjusting.'

Adjusting? I scan the mountain of chaos that's been building over the last week and shake my head. Penthouse Daycare, anyone?

And I thought living with my ex Katie was bad – she had more serums than a pharmacy, took over my closet one hanger at a time, and turned every room into a freaking candle orgy – but I'd take her measured madness over this trainer-flinging, couch-jumping dictator any day of the week. Probably. Maybe.

'I thought you said a few things,' I croak, stepping over a rogue juice carton as I make it to the kitchen unscathed-*ish*. 'This is a full-scale invasion.'

She blows her hair off her flushed face, and I pretend not to notice the way her bottom lip juts out – full, thoughtless, stupidly inviting – or how her oversized sweatshirt slips off one creamy-white shoulder.

'You said we could stay for the summer,' she blurts, yanking my eyes back to hers. 'You didn't say anything about a baggage limit.'

I open my mouth, then close it again as Lottie clambers over my nubuck leather sofa with a delighted shriek, those suspiciously sticky hands every-where all at once.

'But if it's a problem, we can find somewhere else,' she says, tossing the bomb aside so she can snatch a psychedelic backpack from Lottie's fresh grasp just before the kid can hurl it at the wall-mounted TV. 'I *told* Taylor this was too much.'

Taylor's her big sister – well, half-sister. Same shit dad, different mum.

Taylor's also my best friend. Though the best-friend status might be coming under question. I'm not sure what's worse: the whirling dervish of a child or the very unwelcome and entirely prohibited desire I have for her mother.

'Too much?' I repeat, trying to focus while in the background, Lottie giggles and bounces on my furniture like she's auditioning for the toddler Olympics. 'Not at all.'

I didn't think having them move in would turn me into a liar too.

'Look, I know it's not easy having us around,' she says, lifting Lottie into her arms and coming closer, 'especially when you're used to...' She waves a weak hand around.

Peace. Tranquillity. Bachelorhood. All of the above.

'It's fine.'

She stares at me like she doesn't believe me. Hell, *I* don't believe me. But I've made my peace with the temporary situation. It's bachelorhood out, toddler-geddon in. And I'm here for it. Honest.

It's the least I can do for Taylor. The least I can do for Sadie too. After all the girl has endured at the hands of her no-good ex, she deserves a place to lie low and keep out of trouble. But who's going to keep me out of trouble in return?

'Is it safe to get coffee... or is today's plan "death by flying rucksack"?' I grin, making sure she knows I'm teasing.

She blinks, cheeks flaming, making the strip of freckles along the bridge of her nose stand out. Cute. And so not my thing. Meanwhile, *my nose* grows another inch. Bloody Pinocchio.

'Coffee! Yes! Absolutely!' Suddenly, she's far more focused on adjusting the toddler trying to climb her like a deranged koala than on looking at me. 'Very safe. No more projectiles. I don't think.'

'Great.'

She passes me a mug from an overhead cupboard – the glossy black door now sporting more fingerprints than a crime scene – and nods towards the pot. 'There's some ready for you. Extra strong, just how you like it.'

She sets Lottie down on a stool and moves to get the cereal next, rolling onto her toes to reach the top shelf, that damn sweatshirt lifting with her. The tiniest pair of shorts come into view, hugging the globes of her arse like a second skin, and my palms burn. *Fuck.*

Then I feel a very different kind of burn. The kind that comes from a pair of big, blue eyes at waist height, judging me. My eyes flit to Lottie – *yeah, yeah, I know.*

'*Coffee*,' I mutter, hurling myself at the machine and pouring a mugful. 'You want a top up?'

'No, I'm good, ta.'

I turn and lean back against the counter, take a grateful sip. Focus on the rich aroma, the satisfying taste... and *not* the way Sadie's lips press together as her eyes linger on my chest instead of the cereal she's supposed to be pouring.

Tiny wheat hoops make a break for it, scattering across the marble countertop much to Lottie's high-pitched delight.

'Messy mummy!' she giggles, scoffing up the strays within reach.

And I give a soft laugh with her, because truth is, I'm getting a kick out of this mess too. Until I remember all the reasons why I shouldn't.

She's Taylor's little sister. A woman who's been through hell and back courtesy of a man. A woman who's *still* going through hell because of him.

She needs stability and security. Not me, bloody well objectifying her.

One week. Has it really only been a week?

Because if the chaos doesn't kill me, the temptation sure as hell might.

* * *

Sadie

I need to get a grip.

Like, immediately.

Because one more look at Theo Tanner – dark-blond hair a mess, semi-naked body a full-on study in temptation, coffee mug dwarfed by one big hand and those specs giving him a serious and *oh-so* sexy edge – and I'm going to do something monumentally stupid.

Something I swore I would never, ever do again.

Something that breaks the ultimate houseguest rule, and sets the worst possible example for Lottie.

But then...

I've been setting bad examples since the day she was born. Making bad decisions long before then too. It's my forte. Why change now?

I shove some bread in the toaster – anything to keep my eyes off him – and take a breath. Remind myself that I'm *trying* to be better. That I *want* to be better.

For Lottie, as much as for myself.

'Uncle Feo want some?'

From the corner of my eye, I spy her offer out a sticky palm full of cereal hoops and I wait for him to politely decline. This is Theo, after all. Billionaire bachelor Theo. He may have grown up above the corner chippy, feasting off scraps, but these days, he's all about the cold-pressed juice and the caviar. I'm exaggerating, of course... I think.

Instead, he steps forward, his heady scent drifting towards me as he selects one hoop. 'Don't mind if I do.'

He pops it in his mouth and mine hangs open, his exaggerated chew-turned-hum reverberating through my over-sensitised body. Did he just... is he just...?

'Mmm, that's good.'

I think my ovaries just imploded.

Watching the man drink his coffee half-naked is hard enough. Watching him humour my daughter and share her cereal like it's the best part of his morning... It's not just my libido waking up, it's my heart too.

He flicks me a conspiratorial wink before going back in for another and I'm just as spellbound as Lottie.

I swear he doesn't even notice the way he looks, which only makes it worse.

Cocky-hot is one thing. Oblivious-hot is a whole new level of dangerous.

And he's been like this for as long as I can remember. Hot. Unattainable. Taylor's best friend, which means I've been relegated to 'baby sister' since forever... the hanger-on, the one you put up with but don't really notice. Though I forced him to notice me – *really* notice me – seven years ago.

The most embarrassing moment of my life...

I bet he doesn't even remember it, while I wish I could forget. The way my lips bumbled up against his, the heat of him kissing me back, then the searing shame as he leapt away like his life depended on it.

Hell, maybe it did. I certainly died a death that day, and so did the bond I thought we'd built after his dad passed away.

I was the shoulder he cried on. The one person he could be real with. He didn't have to be Theo Tanner: the strong, dependable one. The trader people trusted with their hard-earned cash. The loving son holding it together for his mother. The best friend with all the answers. He was just Theo. The man.

And I loved him for it. More fool me.

Like I said, bad decisions, bad examples – they're my forte. And they all have one thing in common: men.

First Theo, then Danny.

Though saying their names in the same breath feels wrong on every level.

My ex was an abusive prick. Theo... well, Theo just knew better than to want me.

And I should know better than to want him now. Which I *do*. Honest.

He takes another hoop from Lottie, who's now doing her favourite 'one for you, one for me' and I give a flustered laugh. 'You want some milk with those?'

'Nah.' He grins. 'Coffee is perfect.'

'I want coffee!' Lottie declares and Theo chuckles, the sound as invigorating as his hum. More so as his eyes light on mine in question. Does he seriously think I'm about to feed my toddler *coffee*?

Better than him thinking you're ogling the boxers off him!

'I think you already have enough beans in you, kiddo,' he says.

Lottie wrinkles her nose. 'I don't have beans.'

'You do have juice, though,' I say, hunting out the carton I gave her earlier and finding it, complete with juicy puddle on his fancy kitchen floor.

Balls. I swear this place was spotless not ten minutes ago. I made it so. Every surface wiped back to glossy perfection. Every stretch of varnished floor gleaming. Sofa cushions, plumped. Filter coffee set to go.

Then I suggested a nappy change and all hell broke loose. Or rather, *Lottie* did.

We started potty training back in Ireland, but with the chaos of the past few weeks, it's fallen by the wayside. Now she's out of routine and proudly refusing to wear pull-ups, like she's outgrown them entirely.

Which would be great... if I wasn't watching her climb all over his terrifyingly expensive designer sofa with the bladder control of a fruit fly and a glint of rebellion in her eye.

I thrust the carton at her and reach for the cloth at the sink just as Theo moves to refill his coffee, and bam! We collide. Chest to chest. Or, more accurately, my forehead to his bare chest. *Holy smoking...*

Lottie gives a timely, 'Uh-oh!'

'I'm so sorry!' I blurt, jolting back so fast, I slide on the spilled juice and would have perfected the splits if not for Theo's arm shooting around me. He pulls me up against him, saving both me and his coffee that I almost upend in the process.

'You good?' He growls it out, his green eyes as hot as his body pressing into mine.

'Yup.' It's virtually a squeak. Because I'm not. Not even a little.

Not when every bit of me is on high alert, humming like I've licked a battery and his mouth is so close, all I can think about is licking *it*. Which would make my seven-year-old mistake look like a PG blunder.

'Great!' He drops me like a hot potato, which is pretty much how I feel, and goes back to pouring his coffee. Staring at the rich, dark liquid like it holds the answer to his biggest problem. Which, let's be honest, is us.

Meanwhile, Lottie's busy making her juice carton burp.

Thank God someone's keeping it classy around here.

I try to act normal, wipe up the spill and pour milk on Lottie's cereal, but nothing about me is normal. Nothing about this situation is normal. Nothing about my life is normal.

Six years ago, I had it sussed. I met Danny. A guy who made me stop fantasising about the impossible with the man behind me. A guy who loved me and wanted me and whisked me right off my young and naive feet. Fast forward to now, I'm bruised and battered, inside and out, running from one toxic relationship into the home of the man I'd run from in the first place. How's that for a twisted life story?

Taylor would never have suggested I come here if she knew, of course.

My big sis is blissfully unaware of my feelings for Theo. Hell, I wish I was blissfully unaware...

'Are you trying to wear a hole in my floor?'

The bemused murmur comes from just over my shoulder and I die a thousand deaths. *Get a grip, Mercedes!*

I force an easy smile and stand. 'Don't want to leave a sticky residue behind.'

'Tell that to my hallway.'

'Oh God,' I groan. 'Did she get there too?'

'It's no bother, Maggie will see it gone today.'

I frown, swiping a hand through my wild, blonde mop. 'Maggie?'

'My cleaner. She comes every Saturday morning. She's gonna love Lottie.'

I puff. 'You're being sarcastic...'

'I'm not. She'll be torn between work and play. Maggie that is, not Lottie.'

'She shouldn't have to clean up after us. I'll take care of it.'

'You'll do no such thing.' He glances at the view beyond the glass. 'Looks like it's going to be a great day. Why don't you get out, take Lottie to the park?'

I chew on my lip, my eyes drifting to the glorious blue sky stretching over London, and my tummy twists. 'Maybe.'

I won't, but he doesn't need to know that.

The toast pops and I jump in sync, dashing for it while my nerves stay strung up to the ceiling...

* * *

Theo

Sadie plucks the bread from the toaster like she's afraid the thing is still on, and I add another dash of coffee to my very full mug, desperate for something to focus on that isn't her.

Her and thirty seconds of pure, unfiltered temptation pressed up against me.

Jesus.

Less than a minute of contact and my brain short-circuited like a teen crushing on his first girl. Not a man who should know better. A man *way* too old to be crushing on anyone, especially a girl twelve years his junior.

Hell, Taylor's more mum than sister to Sadie, which makes me more... No. Don't go there. Daddy fantasies are *not* my thing. Never have been, never would be—

She leans past me to squeeze the cloth under the tap and so help me God, I almost combust. Coffee sloshes over the side of my mug, and her eyes snap to mine.

'Don't you start making a mess too,' she says with a soft laugh.

Christ, if she only *knew* what kind of mess I had brewing...

I grab the cloth from her hand, careful to minimise any more contact. 'I've got this.'

Only I don't...

'And like I said, Maggie will deal with the cleaning, Sadie.' I finish rinsing the cloth and toss it in the sink. 'Not you.'

And what the hell was with all the 'ies' in his house now. Sadie. Lottie. Maggie. Daddy. I choke on my coffee, and she sends me an arched brow.

'Did I make it too strong?'

'Nope. It's all good.'

It's me that's not.

She moves away, but her expression remains sceptical. The frown between her brows deepening as she butters and cuts the toast into perfect little triangles. I rub the back of my neck.

Just a couple of months, that's all it is. She'll find her feet, move into her own place, and I'll go back to being the highly respected, extremely single, zero-self-control-required bachelor I was before.

Easy.

I take another giant sip and stare stoically at the floor, and not the bare shoulder that's making my mouth wetter than the coffee.

Easy, my arse.

'I'd best get to work.'

Stunning blue eyes hit mine. 'But it's a Saturday?'

I'm already halfway across the kitchen. 'No rest for the wicked.'

And I'm definitely that.

Wicked and perverted and in need of the coldest shower known to man...

'Wicked Uncle Feo!' Lottie calls after me and I swear I hear Sadie stifle a laugh. 'Wicked! Wicked! Wicked!'

Yeah kid, and don't I know it.

* * *

Sadie

I slide the plate of toast to Lottie, weighing up whether to talk her down from using her new favourite word on repeat. But you say something in front of a kid, you're always going to risk it catching on. And I'm sure Theo will take it in his stride. Won't he?

I watch him leave. Sloping off like some shirtless Greek tragedy in nothing more than those black boxer briefs and I know I'm drooling. My logical head screams, *Inappropriate, forbidden, he broke you once and he's gifting you sanctuary now.*

But the woman inside me?

She's already fanning herself with a piece of toast and praying she can make it through the next hour without making the same mistake eighteen-year-old her made.

'Uncle Theo isn't wicked,' I say under my breath. 'Mummy is. And Mummy needs to get this place cleaned up before Maggie arrives...'

I scan the toddler debris which seems to have reached into every corner of Theo's vast, open-plan space – bright pops of chaos against the monochrome backdrop – and press my palm to my head. No wonder the man saw it as a full-on invasion.

'Time to do better at containment, kiddo.'

Impossible, much?

2

SADIE

Seven Years Ago...

'Right, I'm tapping out,' Taylor says, coming to a rolling stop as we hit the edge of the park, 5k into what was supposed to be a 10k run. 'I've got a client in two hours, and this body isn't going to preen itself.'

'Ha! You could show up like that and the guy would probably double your rate,' I say, bouncing from one foot to the other, still high on adrenaline. And I'm not even kidding. She's tall, glossy-black-haired perfection – like if Wonder Woman and Black Widow had a baby, raised it on protein shakes and Pilates, and gave it a supernatural aversion to sweat. Boom: DominaTay!

'Tell her, Theo.'

'Hell no,' he says, shaking his head. 'Too weird.'

'Weird, huh?' Taylor cocks a perfectly manicured brow. 'Thanks.'

'You know what I mean,' he says, hands gripping his hips as he pants for air, his ripped physique in a compression tee making my heart dance harder than the run ever could. 'It'd be like telling my sister I think she's hot.'

'You know we're not blood, right?' I cut in before I can stop myself, aiming for playful but hearing the edge in my own voice. Because the truth is, I'm crushing on him. Hard. Have been for as long as I can remember, and this past year? It's only gotten worse. Watching him unravel after his dad died, seeing the softer, broken parts he let no one else near... it's wrecked me in the best, most irreversible way. I'm hooked. Head over heels.

Twelve-year age gap? Pfft!

He glances at me, his expression unreadable. 'Doesn't make it okay.' Then he looks to my sis. 'Sorry, Tay. Never gonna fancy you.'

'And on that amazing note,' she says, hazel eyes sparkling with laughter, 'I'll see you both later. Try not to kill him, sis. We're not as young as you remember. No matter how much we'd kill to be eighteen again.'

'Geez, Tay. You make yourself sound ancient.'

'After that run, I *feel* ancient. And I need these legs in prime condition for tonight's black-tie gig. *Ciao ciao.*'

She jogs off, ponytail swinging, fingers fluttering high in farewell... and somehow looking more energised than she did ten minutes ago.

'You think she's going off to finish the other 5k alone?' I say.

'If you're asking whether she wanted to escape your pacing, then yes. Completely possible.'

'So why aren't you following her?'

He shrugs, and that grin I know too well tugs at his lips. 'What can I say? Your pacing does it for me. Move it, Gonzales.'

'Gonzales?' I raise a brow.

'Speedy? The cartoon mouse?' He lets out a strangled laugh. 'Ok-ay. Not feeling old. Not feeling old at all...' And then he takes off.

'Hey! Wait up!' I call, grinning as I chase after him.

We settle into a rhythm side by side again, his pace way more brutal than mine ever was.

'So,' he says, after several racing minutes of silence. 'How have things been since you dropped the beauty-school bombshell?'

I roll my eyes. 'She's still pissed. Told me it's not a real career. Which is hilarious, considering she runs an escort agency.'

'She just worries about you.'

'Tell me something I don't know. But she can't have it all her way. She doesn't want me in her business because she doesn't think it's suitable and I—'

He loses his footing and I flick out a hand, stopping just short of his bicep. 'You okay?'

'Yep!' He stares resolutely ahead, jaw clenched. Then, 'You were saying?'

'I can't win. She doesn't want me working for her and she doesn't want me doing my own thing either.'

'She just doesn't want you to leave.'

'Manchester isn't that far.'

'It's far enough when she's used to having you around twenty-four-seven... She'll miss you.'

My eyes flick his way again. 'And what about you, Theo? You gonna miss me too?'

I say it like it's a joke, like it's light and nothing, but it comes out all wrong. Too heavy. Too loaded.

He looks over at me, and the sudden seriousness on his face almost takes my feet out from under me.

'Yes.' His voice is rough, taking on that gruff edge he tries to hide when things get too real, and it makes my heart skip a beat. 'Of course I'll miss you.'

We hit the track that runs down to the river. It's quieter here. Our shortened breaths overlay the kick of gravel beneath our feet, the rush of water, and the wildlife tweeting in the trees. But the only thing I'm attuned to is him.

'I don't know how I would've gotten through this year without you,' he says. 'After Dad... Everyone needed me to hold it together. Mum was a mess. She's still a mess...'

'She'll get there,' I say, hoping I'm right. I love his mum. Everyone does. But for me and Tay, she was the one who put food in our belly when dad was too drunk or distracted to care. She deserves to be happy again.

'As for your sister and Axel...' he says, bringing up his two best friends who should have been there for him, who would have been there for him if he'd given them a chance. 'They'd just given me their life savings to invest. I had to show them I could do it.'

'Which you did and then some.'

He's made a fortune already and it's growing at an exponential rate.

'But with you...'

'You didn't have to be any of that,' I say quietly, accepting my heart's fate with it.

'Yeah. You never needed me to be anything but me, and I don't think I ever thanked you.'

He slows to a stop, turning into me as I do the same.

'You don't need to thank me,' I say. 'You've been there for me too. For as long as I can remember... you and Tay have had my back.'

A soft smile touches his lips. 'Ever the humble one, aren't you?'

His hand lifts, and with the lightest touch, he sweeps the hair from my face. His fingers linger behind my ear, his unguarded gaze sears mine.

'And for what it's worth, I'm happy you're going after your dreams. You deserve them all.'

His hand falls away slowly – like he doesn't want to let me go – and I swear he's breathing faster. My pulse thrums in my throat as we just stand there, staring at each other. His eyes flick to my mouth. My stomach twists, flips, tightens with hope.

He finally sees me. Not as Tay's little sister. Not as a kid. He sees... *me*.

And then I lean in without thinking, brushing my lips against his. It's barely a kiss, more a question I don't know how to ask. And for one breathless second, he doesn't respond, doesn't move, and my heart plummets.

But then... he catches it, his mouth crashing into mine in sudden answer.

His hands slide to my waist, pulling me in. He parts my lips with his tongue and the sudden invasion makes my head spin and my body melt, my moan as wild and wanton as I feel.

And then – just like that – he jerks back. Breath ragged. Eyes wild.

'Shit!' The curse cuts like a blade as his hands plunder his hair. 'Forgive me, I shouldn't have! What the fuck was I thinking?'

'Forgive you?' My voice shakes. 'I kissed you!'

'I kissed you back!'

'So? I— I love you Theo.'

His eyes flare. 'No. No, you don't.'

'I do. I've loved you for—'

'You don't love me,' he snaps back. 'You can't.'

'But I do.'

'You only think you do. You're too young, you're—'

A laugh tears through my throat. 'I'm old enough to know my own heart.'

'Not when you think you're in love with me.'

'Why is it so hard to believe?'

'Because I'm the one guy you've had in your life since you were five. I was the one you came to when you scraped your knee in the park. Or fell out with your friends at school. I was the one you came to when you needed a man to make it all better.'

'Jesus.' I stumble back a step, the meaning of his words landing with a sickening thud. 'You think I have daddy issues?'

'No— *Jesus*, fuck, no.' He slams another hand through his hair, face pinched and pale. 'Hell, maybe. I don't know. Even before he died, your father was never—'

'What the *fuck*, Theo?'

'I'm not trying to be a dick, Sadie. But you're eighteen. You're—'

'Stop.' I cut him off, my voice trembling, my eyes burning. 'It's bad enough that Taylor still talks to me like I'm some helpless kid, but you?' My voice cracks. 'I thought you saw me.'

'I do,' he says softly. 'I do see you.'

'No.' I shake my head, tears stinging at my eyes. 'You don't.'

He opens his mouth to say something, but I don't want to hear it, and so I run as fast as my heart is breaking.

He doesn't come after me.

Not then. Not in all the years since.

And I don't look back... or at least, I try not to.

3

THEO

'How are things?'

I can sense the frown in Taylor's voice all the way down the phone.

'Things are fine,' I lie, plucking a stuffed narwhal off my desk and studying its fluffy, pink tusk with a bemused smile.

'Then why isn't she answering her phone?'

'You're asking the wrong person.'

'Theo, I'm serious. I think she's avoiding my calls.'

'Why would she do that?'

'Because... because she thinks I'm fussing.'

'And are you?'

'She's my baby sister, she's been my responsibility since I was fifteen years old and I gave her space once, look how that ended. I'm not about to make the same mistake again.'

'She's still a grown woman, Tay.'

Not the thing I should be saying, not to Taylor and not to myself. I'm all too aware of Sadie's womanly status and willing myself to become unaware ASAP. It's why I've been locked in my study for the best part of the weekend. Anything to avoid a repeat of the kitchen-collision yesterday morning...

'...it's not right I'm telling you.'

I tune back into what Taylor's saying and whole-heartedly agree, even though I know we're referring to very different things. At least I hope we are.

I wasn't exactly listening to whatever she'd been saying after I went down the grown-woman tangent, but I'm pretty sure it had nothing to do with my disobedient cock that keeps springing up like some malfunctioning jack-in-the-box.

'What isn't?'

'Theo! Can you get your head out of your work for one minute and concentrate?'

She says 'work', I hear 'pants' and it's enough to have me sitting straighter.

'Sorry.' I spin away from the screens churning out numbers and pull my head from the gutter. 'You were saying?'

'It's wrong that she didn't feel she could come to me when she needed me the most.'

'She came to you, Tay.' I get to my feet, taking the little narwhal with me. I've no idea how the stuffed animal got in my study but as with anything of Lottie's, things just migrate. 'She wouldn't be in my home now if she hadn't.'

'Not when it all started, when I could have done something to get her out of there. Before he got his claws into her and messed with her head. She isn't the same girl any more, and she won't tell me what happened, not in detail, but...'

'Hey, will you quit berating yourself for this.' I walk up to the glass and take in the snaking Thames below, focus on the familiar sight rather than the unknown. Because the unknown will only send my head down the same road as Taylor, imagining the worst and wondering if I could have saved her from it. 'You did what you could, when you could. It wasn't your fault she fell in love with that piece of shit.'

'Yeah, well, until that piece of shit is behind bars, I won't rest.'

'And the cops are on the case, so is Axel...'

Axel's our business partner, our best friend since he stepped between us and the neighbourhood gang when we were thirteen. From postcode wars to boardroom floors, council estates to the *Sunday Times* Rich List, we've made it. Ask anyone and they'll tell you: I'm the brains, Taylor's the beauty, and Axel's the brawn.

But the truth's far more nuanced than that.

These days, I head up investments. Taylor runs the clubs. Axel handles security. It's a mix that works. Billionaires before forty. Winning at life.

Though I know that only adds to Taylor's guilt now. To have all that money, all that power, and still not have saved Sadie from the hell that was her ex...

I glance down, suddenly aware of the bobbing narwhal in my hand. I'm using a stuffed mammal as a stress ball – go figure. But Sadie's ex has me damn near ready to punch something. Preferably him.

'How is she?' Taylor asks. 'Truthfully.'

'How do you think?' I deflect, because what the hell do I know? I can't spend more than a few minutes around her without bolting. Chaos or temptation – both are killing off my sanity. 'Why don't you ask her?'

'I would if she'd pick up the phone.'

'I'm sure she's just busy.'

'Doing what?'

'Chasing down a kid, for a start. Those things run on never-ending batteries. Energizer should have trademarked toddlers, not bunnies.'

'That's my niece you're talking about.'

'And? I'm simply stating a fact.'

'So, she's okay, she's getting out with Lottie, doing stuff?'

'Like?'

'I don't know, normal stuff, the kind of stuff you do with a kid.'

I think back over the week, and it's always me saying goodbye. Leaving on business, going for a run, meeting up with Axel...

Guilt starts to worm its way in. She could have gone out while I was out, though. But somehow, I suspect she hasn't. She's always around, either grappling with Lottie, or tapping away on her phone or her laptop.

I guess I could have asked her. Shown an interest.

Hell, I could have taken them out, done something with them, made them feel more welcome. Instead, I've been too focused on running the other way. Running from my guilt, the attraction, and a seven-year-old memory I can't seem to bury. A kiss that was as wrong back then as it would be now. But every replay of those innocent lips moving over mine and it's hello jack!

'Theo?'

'I don't know,' I admit, staring up at the clear blue sky outside and recalling how yesterday had been just as nice. The perfect day to get out. And I'd told her just the same. To forget the cleaning and go. But had she? No. 'It's only been a week, she probably just needs time to settle in first, get her bearings again...'

'A week stuck inside a penthouse, shit. Lottie must be climbing the walls.'

Now that I could answer a hundred times over. 'I'd say so.'

'You can't keep a kid cooped up like that.'

Guilt morphs into the defensive. 'I did tell you my place was hardly ideal.'

'It beats her worrying about bringing trouble to my door.'

'So, it's okay for her to bring trouble my way?' I quip, then instantly regret it.

Where the hell's my famed cool?

Apparently, it packed up and left the day Sadie moved in.

'Of course not. But Danny's too self-absorbed to know you exist. And at least you're at home. I'm away so much and I don't want her on her own. Not right now and not while that prick is still out there somewhere. I sleep easier knowing you're keeping an eye on her.'

Yeah, I'm doing that all right. If the narwhal could squeak, it just did.

'She needs to get out though, Theo. He kept her caged long enough. She needs to start living her life again...'

'She can't be afraid of running into him here. He's back in Ireland. She's in London. She's safe. Free to come and go and do whatever makes her happy.'

It comes out tight as I reel with the truth. She hadn't been any of those things. Free. Safe. Happy.

'I hope so, but—' She breaks off as another woman's voice comes down the line, muffled, distant. Her PA? 'Give me one sec, Theo.'

'Sure.'

I turn away from the view, my need to see happy-smiley, very safe Sadie overriding any sense of self-preservation as I leave my study and seek her out. I follow the faint sound of toddler to her wing of my apartment, half-expecting trip hazards or plastic landmines, but everything's oddly... neat. *Too* neat.

Had she really taken my *invasion* joke to heart?

Her door is open just a crack, so I tap lightly. No answer. Just Lottie's voice carrying through in a sing-song ramble only a three-year-old could invent.

She can't need privacy if the door's ajar, right?

I step inside, straight into what looks like a toddler boot camp designed by chaos theorists. If the rest of my place looks bare, it's because every last toy, book, blanket, squeaky thing has upped and landed here. All except the narwhal-slash-stress ball still clutched in my hand.

'Uncle Feo!' Lottie's straight ahead of me in the en suite, perched in front of the toilet on a potty, a book in her lap, and stickers – *so many stickers* – everywhere. The glossy tiled floor, walls, sink, her hair, her cheeks...

Welcome to the Ministry of Mayhem.

Population: one very small dictator, complete with throne.

Where in the hell is Sadie?

'Wan' one?' Lottie says, lifting out a sticker-clad finger.

'Remind me again why she couldn't stay at Axel's?' I murmur into the phone as I give Lottie a grin as tight as my grip.

'Are you really asking me that again?' Taylor says, coming back on the line.

'Sure am.' Because my question is perfectly reasonable. Axel's the muscle. The protector. The human equivalent of a security system with abs. If anyone should be keeping Sadie and her kid safe from her walking-red-flag of an ex, it's him. Not me.

'I thought I'd explained that well enough.'

Oh, she has. Repeatedly. With charts, probably. The thing is, Axel isn't just our best friend and business partner, he's also the biggest player known to man.

'He wouldn't touch her,' I say, while telling myself to listen up. 'She's your sister.'

Taylor gives an unladylike snort. 'She's a woman first.'

Yeah, and don't I know it.

'What did you just say?'

Fuck, did I say that out loud?

I drag a hand through my hair. 'You act like he can't control himself.'

'Have you ever known a woman not to fall into bed with him?'

She has a point, but... 'You haven't.'

'Because I know better.'

'Ri-ight,' I drawl.

'*And* I know better than to risk a lifelong friendship for what can only be a few minutes of fun.'

Hell, I should be taking notes and reminding myself of the very same, daily if not hourly. Along with the hefty reminder that Taylor *trusts* me because I'm *not* Axel.

But what if she knew that Sadie was the one woman capable of making me be more Axel...

'A few minutes?' I say, moving forward to take the sticker Lottie's now frantically waving at me before she tumbles off the potty. 'I'll tell him you said that.'

'You wouldn't dare.'

'Said what?'

I release my grip on the narwhal as Sadie steps through the dressing-room doors to my right, and the toy lands with a silent thud that mirrors the dive my gut just took.

For the first time in a week, I curse my penthouse for all things noise-cancelling and cubby-holing because she must have been in the room all along. And now I can't remember what I've said on this side of the convo and what she'll infer and...

'Gotta go, Tay.'

'Is Sadie there?' she rushes to ask. 'Can you put her on?'

I glance at Sadie and she's shaking her head.

'I'll get her to call you back.'

I'm already hanging up the phone.

Taylor's concern can wait.

The look in Sadie's eye can't.

* * *

Sadie

I wasn't trying to eavesdrop.

But after the kitchen fiasco yesterday – and barely a glimpse of him since – having Theo suddenly stroll into the bedroom, the one place I've been obsessively trying to keep 'us' contained in after his *invasion* remark, felt like a bad joke at my expense.

It took several breaths to come to my senses, another to find my voice.

And now he's standing there, looking just as stunned as I was.

'I'll get it cleaned up,' I hurry to assure him as I race towards Lottie, head down, cheeks hot. If I had any doubts about Theo's feelings on us staying, I don't now. 'I just needed to get her some fresh clothes.'

'Hey, hold up!' He catches my arm as I rush past – his touch barely there, but it crackles through me like a live wire, arresting me mid-stride, arresting my gaze too. 'I didn't mean that.'

Our gazes lock, and I wish to God I could look away, but my damned body won't obey.

'Which bit exactly?'

And now it seems I can't control my tongue either... In the background, Lottie is humming along to Princess Pee Pee, thankfully oblivious to our little exchange. Though I keep my voice down just in case.

Her father resented her enough, I don't want her thinking Theo does too.

'The bit where you accused us of invading, or the bit where you asked my sister why Axel couldn't be stuck with us instead?'

'I didn't say—'

'You didn't have to.'

'But I didn't mean—'

'I've known you most of my life, Theo, you always say what you mean.' Kiss-gate being a prime example. 'It's the one thing you're exceptional at...'

And who am I kidding? The *one* thing? This man is exceptional at many, many things – looking good being right up there with the rest.

'It's not how you think it is.'

'Then why don't you tell me exactly how it is?'

His eyes dip over my face, my chest... I can feel the band of exposed skin between my cropped tank and my shorts prickling under the weight of his stare, my nipples following suit, and then his eyes launch back to mine.

'Better still, let's go out.'

A laugh bubbles up within me. Surely, I didn't hear him right. '*Out?*'

We've been living with the guy for a week, and this is the first time he's mentioned going anywhere together... Hell, he doesn't even eat meals with us!

'Sure. The sun is shining. We can take Lottie to Hyde Park, get some ice cream...'

'Ice cream?' My mini devil has bat ears when her favourite food is mentioned, and now she's giving me those big baby blues. 'I want ice cream!'

'There we go, Lottie's up for it.' He gives me a shameless grin. 'So, what do you say?'

I'm still floundering over his sudden turnaround – from wishing me gone to asking us out. What's he playing at? Or rather, what's Taylor playing at? Because I have no doubt that she's behind this.

'I don't know,' I say. 'I'm trying to get back on track with Lottie's potty training...'

'And going out will get in the way of that?' he says, eyes narrowed.

'It's almost Lottie's lunchtime,' I counter.

'Concierge will sort us a picnic.'

'I really don't fancy tackling the Tube on a day like today.'

'Who said anything about the Tube? We're taking my car.'

God, the man has an answer for everything...

'You'll never get parked.'

'My driver will drop us and come back when we're done.'

His *driver*?

Of course he has a driver, stupid. He's a bloody billionaire. As wealthy as Taylor. It's just you who's skint and having to start over.

'How long do you need to get ready?'

'I— *What*?' Were they seriously doing this?

'I assume you'll need to prep a bag for the sticker monster.' He sends Lottie a wink that sends a stream of butterflies through my already dancing belly. 'Twenty minutes? Thirty?'

'Twenty's fine,' I say weakly.

'Great.'

And then he sweeps out like the giant, sexy, frustratingly disruptive tornado that he is. And he thinks *we're* the Masters of Chaos?!

I look at Lottie, who's already tossed her book aside and is tugging up today's choice of training pants with about as much glee as the dread I feel...

It'll be okay. You're in company. Danny doesn't know where you are, and there's an ocean between you both now.

Though he could be on the other side of the world, and it wouldn't be far enough. Because it's not even him per se. It's the ghost of him.

'Mummy, 'm stuck!'

I zone in on Lottie, who is twirling on the spot, trying to get her arm through her romper suit, and shake myself out of my funk. 'Coming, baby.'

Hyde Park will be *nice*. Hyde Park will be *fun*.

No harm will come to us.

No harm at all.

Save for the kind inspired by being up close and personal with Theo for the day...

4

THEO

Note to self: next time you suggest going out in the car, get in the front with Shaun.

It turns out the rear seat is no place for two adults and a booster. Not if you want to keep more than an inch between you and the woman you can't look at without wondering what her lips taste like now.

Who knew a kid's car seat took up more space than Dwayne 'The Rock' Johnson? No wonder Sadie glanced at me all wide-eyed when I followed her in. And it wasn't like I did it out of habit either.

I did it to reassure her that I *want* to be doing this. That I want to spend time in their orbit – and that they're welcome in mine – even if I haven't exactly shown it to date.

But judging by the way her legs are pressed tight together, her palms stuck between them, and her eyes stare resolutely ahead, she's finding this about as easy as I am.

'You really didn't have to do this,' she says through her teeth.

Lottie glances between us, not really hearing her mother but sensing her speaking. Her true focus is on the tablet Aunt Tay-Tay bought her. She grips its neon-pink case like it might vanish if she blinks, while her glittery headphones mercifully muffle whatever high-pitched drama the animated blobs are unleashing.

'I'm sure you have better things to be doing with your Sunday.'

'I wanted to do it,' I say, and I can practically hear her silent scoff.

'I did, Sades.'

She turns to me, one brow raised, and I strip my sunglasses to hold her gaze.

'I swear it.'

Tension coils through her frame. Her blue eyes bright as they dig into mine, hunting for the lie, but I'm too hooked on hers to care. I could sit here for days. Work be damned.

'So...' Her tongue flicks across her bottom lip – something I really *didn't* need to witness this close. 'Taylor didn't put you up to it?'

Fuck.

'It's too nice a weekend to spend it indoors,' I hedge. 'And if I'm being totally honest, I feel bad that I didn't offer to take you out sooner.'

All true.

'You feel bad?' she huffs out. 'Pull the other one.'

I choke on a laugh. More surprised that she's calling me out on it. No one calls me out on anything. Save for Taylor and Axel, who know me better than I know myself at times. But then, this is Sadie, the girl who always saw right through me...

'Why is that so hard to believe?'

She hesitates, her blue eyes sweeping over my face. Then she shakes her head and turns away, and the scent of her shampoo – sweet and subtle, cherry, if I had to guess – rises in the air like a hit of high-end perfume. One my body's all too eager to enjoy, even as my brain labels it: *Bad Idea No. 5.*

'You shouldn't feel bad. You're a busy man doing us a favour by giving us a place to stay,' she murmurs, her eyes now fixed on Lottie's screen. 'But you can quit with the babysitting, okay?'

'The *baby*sitting?'

She might as well have kicked me in my overly stoked balls for the sickening roll in my gut.

'You think I don't know that she asked you to take us in so that you could keep an eye on us? That she didn't guilt trip you into this now so that she could make sure we're getting out and about, having fun, living life' – she does finger quotes around the words – 'so that she can feel better about this whole situation?'

'It's not about *her* feeling better,' I say tightly. 'It's about *you* feeling better.'

'Perhaps.'

'There's no "perhaps" about it. She loves you. She loves you both. She wants you to be able to put the past behind you and get on with your life. Is that really so bad?'

'It is if you're wishing Axel was the man she'd put in your place.'

'I didn't say I wished—'

She clenches her hands together in her lap, her stress ripping through me, and I give up on the semantics of it. She needs the truth. A version of it at least.

'Can you blame me, Sadie? Seriously?'

'Wow,' she scoffs, 'I think I preferred it when you were at least trying to deny it.'

'Axel *is* the guy who should be looking out for you. He's the one with the security company. He's the one who used to work the doors long before he became the top dog. If any one of us should be keeping you safe from that piece of shit, it's him.'

But above all, Axel's not the one haunted by the ghost of her mouth on his – by the one kiss that never should have happened and the thousand I haven't stopped imagining since.

That wasn't to say Axel *wouldn't* imagine it though, given a chance. Imagine it *and* act on it. And that thought doesn't make me feel any better either.

'Are you saying you're not up to the task?'

She looks at me now, eyes lit with challenge, a teasing glint that slices straight through to my pride. She's testing me – my ability, my masculinity – and damn if my body doesn't bristle at the idea while thriving on her sudden fire.

'I'm saying that of the two of us, Axel is the more obvious choice.'

'Well, when you put it like that...' she says, lips twisting wryly.

'Not to mention you could've just as easily gone to Taylor's. It blows my mind she sent you to me when she has a place in the city big enough for you both. I know she's away a lot, but Axel would've put someone on you twenty-four-seven if need be.'

And just like that, the fire in her dies, and I know I've hit another nerve. Big mouth!

'Look Sadie, it's—'

'She didn't tell you?' she says quietly, her left knee starting to bob.

'Tell me what?'

'Why she didn't want me with her...'

'She told me that you didn't want to risk Danny beating down her door. That you couldn't cope with her fussing, too.'

She's nodding but her knee keeps jigging.

'What else is there?' Because I know there's more; I've known it all along. But when Taylor asks for a favour, I do it. No question. 'Sade—'

'She didn't tell you that we fought?'

'What— no? When?'

She wrings her hands, shakes her head. 'It doesn't matter. Not any more.'

'It does if you're still—'

'Sorry to interrupt, sir,' Shaun says from the front. 'But we're here. Do you want me to pull over?'

No. I want to tell him to keep driving until I get the whole sorry tale out of Sadie, but I know that'd probably freak her out even more.

'Please, Shaun.' I look back at her. 'We'll pick this up later.'

'There's nothing to pick up,' she says, avoiding my eye. 'It was a stupid argument. It happened a long time ago. She said some things. I said some things. And things haven't been the same since. I doubt they ever will be. End of story.'

The car rolls to a stop, and she quickly moves to unbuckle her seatbelt, her fingers electrifying my hip as she fumbles over the button. 'Now can we get out of here, please?'

'Wait.'

I cover her hands – partly to stop the accidental caress from lighting me up any further, and partly because I need a second to process what she just said.

She and Taylor were inseparable. From the moment Sadie's mum left her on their dad's doorstep and disappeared, they came as a unit.

Yes, Sadie left with Danny. Yes, the distance must've been brutal.

But a fight?

Bad enough to crack that bond?

And why the hell hasn't Taylor told me about it?

'Sadie?'

* * *

Sadie

Theo reaches out when I don't look at him, his finger light upon my chin. No touch should be this dizzying. No gaze, no scent, no man!

He eases my chin up until I have no choice but to meet his eye. Theo semi-naked is drop-dead gorgeous, Theo broody and commanding – *dynamite.*

'We *will* talk about this later, okay?'

No. Not okay. I swallow. It's hard enough acknowledging how I feel about it, to put words to it and have him judge me too. No, thanks. But I can't force the words past my lips.

And then his eyes are *on* my lips and I'm about two seconds away from spontaneously combusting.

'Okay,' I hear myself agree. But honestly, there's nothing I wouldn't give him when he looks at me like that – those green eyes hotter than the sun blazing outside.

'Good.'

It comes out raw, breathless, just like I feel. His gaze drifts back up, his mouth parting as he wets the inner edge of his lip. Oh. My. *God.* The space between us shrinks, and I can't breathe. I can't move. I can't—

'Eeeee!' Lottie screeches, straining at her harness like a caged gremlin, her tablet thudding into my lap as I jerk back – moment shattered. Thank God.

'Mummy! Out!'

'Okay, honey, okay.'

I throw myself into freeing her, wrestling with the harness like I've never used one before, while Theo steps out, smooth and composed – like his world hasn't just tilted the way mine has.

And let's face it, it hasn't. This is all on me. *In* me. The woman who should know better...

Once burned, twice shy? I wish.

The door opens beside Lottie and Theo reaches in. 'The park awaits you, princess.'

She lets out an excited squeal and thrusts her headphones at me before launching herself into his arms – easy as – and I feel the smallest pinch of envy.

Oh, to be that trusting again...

Oh, to be able to do that with Theo again...

'Can I help you with your bag?' Shaun says, glancing over his shoulder at a very frozen me.

'Nope— nope, I've got it,' I say, cheeks burning as I shove Lottie's things into her bag and scramble out of the backseat, careful not to get taken out by passing cars as I step onto the road and close the door behind me.

It's the noise that hits me first: the constant hum and clatter of city life. Horns. Barking. Shouting. Then comes the heat – thick and pressing, clinging to my skin.

I join Theo and Lottie on the pavement, my eyes darting all around. Even with the shade being gifted by the trees lining the park and the tall, fancy buildings across the way, the air feels too hot, too thin.

At least I dressed light – trainers, shorts, vest – but sweat still gathers between my breasts, at the bend of my elbows, the nape of my neck... I drop Lottie's bag to the ground and tug a bobble from my wrist, use it to scrape my hair into a high ponytail and breathe. Once. Twice.

'You okay?'

I blink. Theo's watching me, a crease between his brows as he sets Lottie on her feet and swings the picnic holdall over his shoulder.

I nod.

I'm not.

But he doesn't need to know my heart is skittering like it's got somewhere else to be – and this time, it's not all for him.

So much for a relaxing day outdoors...

I take Lottie's hand as she starts to move off, and Theo hoists her bag onto the same shoulder as the holdall. He's in a plain white tee and navy cargo shorts – very much the unassuming billionaire on a rare day off – but the sight of that sparkly unicorn bag slung across his tall, lean frame makes my already-pounding heart beat louder.

Somehow, I manage a smile I almost feel.

'Suits you,' I say, aiming for a tease – anything to make this moment feel as light as it should. 'But I can carry it.'

'I've got it,' he says, flashing a grin that does a much better job of warming me through. Surprise, surprise. 'Despite what you were suggesting in the car,' he adds, slotting on a cap and pulling his shades from the collar of his tee, 'I'm man enough to go full-on princess when required.'

Lottie smothers a giggle with her palm. 'Uncle Feo makes the *best* princess.'

'Better than Mummy?' I ask, mock offended.

She considers me with a furrowed brow, then declares with a nod, 'Mummy is the prettiest!'

'She's not wrong,' Theo murmurs – so quiet, so sure, it makes my head snap up. But he's already looking away, shades on, gaze fixed on the park entrance like he didn't just knock something loose inside my chest.

I don't get a chance to dwell on it. Lottie's already tugging me forward, skipping behind a family of four – two kids, two parents, all holding hands. Maybe it's that image that inspires her, or maybe it's just Theo, but she reaches for his hand too, planting herself between us like she's done it a hundred times before.

He doesn't even miss a beat, just folds his fingers gently around hers and keeps on walking.

And suddenly, we're a trio. A unit. Strolling into Hyde Park like we belong together.

My heart gives another exaggerated beat.

A beat that refuses to settle as we get deeper into the park. All around us, the noise shifts and builds. The trees rustle sharply in the breeze, bikes clatter past, a busker twangs on his guitar, dogs bark, children scream. It all comes at me, no space between one sound and the next. No pause. Just pressure.

I can feel my shoulders inching up, my body folding inward – shrink and shield.

That is, until Lottie lets out an excited squeal and I jolt, every one of my limbs springing free.

'Swans, Mummy! Look!'

She releases Theo's hand to point wildly at the birds gathered at the water's edge ahead, their white feathers gleaming like beacons in the glaring summer sun.

'I see them, kiddo,' I say, forcing a smile, and Theo glances my way.

'Are you sure you're okay?'

I nod but my smile wavers at the edges. My heart's still pounding – too hard, too fast. I wipe one sweaty palm against my denim shorts, keep the other locked around Lottie's hand as my eyes flick left, right...

A group of teenagers erupt into laughter. One of them shouts something unintelligible at the top of his lungs and I flinch, instinctively pulling Lottie closer. The sound filters through me like broken glass, a memory I can't fight off coming to the fore.

Another hot day, but a different city, a different park, *all* the people. Danny had been out with friends the night before. He was a cheerful drunk, but a hungover Danny was the worst kind of mean. Knowing he'd be dead to the world till noon, I slipped out with Lottie, hoping for just a little peace.

We were on the swings when he showed up. I still remember the look on his face – rage so sharp, I fell back before he even touched me. He yanked me to him without a word, his grip bruising, dragging me home as he shouted every name he could think of. 'Slut' was his favourite that day. My dress was too low, too short – was I trying to get attention? Did I *want* men staring at what was his?

That was the last time I ever took Lottie out to enjoy the sunshine.

A breeze cuts through the heat, provoking the goosebumps now rife across my skin. I blink, and Hyde Park snaps back into focus – sun-drenched and full of life. It's a place I once loved, pre-Danny. A place I *should* love again.

But the noise keeps pressing in, the bad memories drowning out the good as I shiver and Theo quits walking.

'Sadie?'

He strips his sunglasses to frown down at me, his eyes searching mine.

I wonder how well he sees me without the lenses.

'Do you want to find somewhere quieter?' he asks.

Well enough, apparently.

Maybe he's wearing contacts.

Maybe those sunglasses aren't prescription at all.

Or maybe those brilliant-green eyes don't need any aid to see me – really see me – right now?

Funny, the things your brain fixates on when you're trying to talk yourself down from a panic attack. But his eyes could distract me from a gazillion things – the suffocating feeling in my chest being right up there with the churn in my gut.

Still, I hesitate.

I don't want to ruin the day.

I don't want to ruin *Lottie's* day. She's so happy to be out in the sun, to be somewhere new and exciting, and I know this is what she needs. What I need too. If not fun, at least a taste of normality.

The kind of normality that isn't shaped by terror.

'I'm fine,' I say eventually, one hand stroking Lottie's soft curls, the other gripping her tiny hand like an anchor.

'I don't believe you,' he says gently, the concern in his gaze holding me hostage and I abandon the act with the smallest shake of my head.

'I hate that this happens,' I admit, voice barely above a whisper. It makes me so angry that Danny still has this kind of power over me. We haven't been together in months. I haven't seen him since his last explosion, the one that finally pushed me to go to the Gardaí and get the restraining order. That was a whole month ago. But he's ingrained in my soul, like a stain I can't scrub clean.

Perhaps if they'd been able to hunt him down, arrest him, do something...

'Is it the crowds, the noise...?'

I swallow hard, taking in the familiar surroundings – the lush green trees, the historic Serpentine Bridge, the lake dotted with boats and birds, people everywhere enjoying a day out in the sun... just as I would have. Before.

'We can go somewhere else if you like?'

I shake my head and bring my eyes back to his. 'No, I want to stay. I used to love coming here. I want to love it again.' Hell, I want to love life again. 'Lottie will love it too,' I say, stronger now, more determined. Because ultimately, that's what matters most. My daughter and her happiness. A real childhood.

He's studies me – quietly, intensely – the grooves either side of his mouth deepening with his thoughts. I wish I knew what he was thinking.

Then again... maybe I don't.

He probably thinks I'm a few fries short of a happy meal.

And honestly? He'd be right.

I look down at Lottie. She's nestled herself between my legs, caught somewhere between excitement and nerves. I bet she's picking up on my mood too and I hate that. Her fingers have found their way into her mouth – a pacifying habit I should probably help her drop. But if I had something that soothed me so easily, I wouldn't be giving it up anytime soon either.

Unless that pacifier was Theo-shaped... and oh how easy it would be to let that happen.

'I have an idea,' the man himself says, catching my gaze. 'Row or peddle?'

'Huh?'

He grins as he slips his glasses back on and gestures to the blue boats and pedaloes floating on the lake. 'It'll be quieter out there, but you'll still get to enjoy the park, and Lottie can play Captain.'

Mini-me's head snaps up. 'Me? Captain!'

'Okay,' I say, my daughter's excitement nearly contagious. 'What's it to be then, Captain Lottie? Are we rowing a boat or pedalling like a bicycle?'

'Rowing!' she blurts.

'Very well,' I say with a real smile. 'The princess has spoken.'

'No princess, Mummy! Captain!'

I ruffle her hair. 'So you are, honey— *I mean*, Captain.'

'In that case, let's go secure your vessel, Captain!' Theo declares for Lottie's benefit, but that damn grin is aimed squarely at me. 'Just so long as Mummy's absolutely certain?'

The only thing I'm certain of is that his grin still makes my heart skip, and his charm slips past every wall I've built. He's lifting my mood, reeling me back in – like he hasn't already been the mistake I swore I wouldn't make twice.

'Lead the way, sailor.'

But I'm not dropping anchor in Heartbreak Bay.

Not this time.

No way, José.

5

SADIE

Five Years Ago

I'm lugging the heaviest box known to man, but it's nothing compared to the weight of my sister's stare.

She stands there like she's got it all figured out, like she knows exactly what's best – for me, for her, for everyone. Only, she doesn't.

Worse still, she puts on this tough front, wants the world to see her as unshakeable, unbreakable, only she's not.

I can see the hurt in her eyes, the fear too, and I hate that I put it there.

But she won't listen. And I *do* have to go.

Danny's outside with the engine running. He's already hit the horn twice and I don't blame him. We've got a ferry to catch and hundreds of miles ahead. This was meant to be a flying visit to grab my things and say goodbye. But Tay's acting like she's never going to see me again, and she's not letting me go without a fight.

It's like the beauty-school showdown, only this time, it's getting personal.

And I don't like it. Not one bit.

'Sis, please don't do this,' I say, wanting to hug her, kiss her, and walk out the door knowing she'll be okay, that we're okay.

'No, you don't do this,' she fires back. 'You barely know him.'

'We've been together a year. Long enough to know that I want this.'

'But Ireland?'

'It's his home.'

'This is your home.'

It hasn't really been my home for two years now. Manchester has. I threw my all into making a new life up there, one that allowed me to put the whole mortifying incident with Theo behind me. And it's where I met Danny and he's amazing. He makes me feel seen. Special. Loved. And...

'I love him, Tay.'

'No. You don't.'

I choke on a laugh. 'I think I know how I feel.'

She folds her arms, her fingers biting into her skin. 'You only think you're in love because—' She breaks off abruptly, her eyes shimmering with whatever she won't say.

'Because?' I press, dread becoming a living, breathing thing in my gut.

'Because you're desperate to be loved.'

I stare back at her, my heart twisting with my gut.

'You don't know what you're talking about,' I say quietly.

'I do, honey.' She steps towards me, hand outstretched, and I shift away.

'You don't!'

'I've seen it your whole life. You chased scraps from Dad. Clung to friends who didn't care. You remember Miss Winters, in primary school? You sobbed for days when she went on maternity leave and never came back.'

'I was seven, Tay.'

'And then there was Theo.'

The box slips in my grip. 'What about Theo?'

She wets her lips, her eyes penetrating mine and I swear, I'm going to puke.

'The way you lit up when he came over. The way you followed him around like he hung the moon...'

Humiliation claws through me, burning hot behind my ribs, my cheeks, my eyes.

'You grew out of the blushing. But it was always there. It's textbook abandonment stuff.'

Abandonment! First, daddy issues from Theo, and now this from Tay. I'm not having it.

'If anyone's got abandonment issues here, it's you!' I throw back at her.

'You're the one who can't let me go! You're the one suffocating me, refusing to let me move on.'

'Because Danny's not right for you.'

'You don't even know him!'

'I've seen him around you enough to know his type. He's possessive. Controlling. Jealous—'

'Like looking in a mirror, then.'

'What's that supposed to mean?'

'You just described yourself.'

'I'm not jealous of you, Sadie.'

'No,' I say, bitterness spilling out. 'Just of Danny for taking me away from you.'

'I just want what's best for you.'

'And he is what's best for me. He loves me.'

'That's not love.'

'And what would you know about it? You've never had a relationship last longer than five minutes. You hop from one bed to another, and you say I'm the one desperate to be loved? At least I don't go around behaving like a—'

I break off but the meaning lands like a slap to her flawless cheek. She stiffens, her face paler than pale. But hell, if she wants to stand there telling me how I should live my life, I can sure as shit do the same.

'You can think what you like about me, but I love you, Sadie. And I don't want to fight with you. You're my little sister. You're the only good thing Dad ever gave me, and I will always want to protect you and look out for you.'

'I love you too. But you don't have to do any of that any more. I have Danny now. And I want that for me. I want love. I want a family. A real one. Not the fucked-up mess we had.'

She swallows hard. 'And what about college? Your diploma?'

'I thought you'd be pleased I'm sacking it off.'

'Sadie, that's not—'

'I have my vlog now. I don't need the diploma.'

'You mean you have him, don't you? You're giving it all up for him?'

'And so what if I am? It's my decision to make, not yours.'

'Don't you mean mistake?'

'For God's sake, Tay, I'm trying to—'

The horn blares again and I wince.

'I should go before Old Man Leo takes his sweeping brush to Danny's car.'

I step up to her, angling the box away as I lean in on tiptoes and kiss her frozen cheek. 'I'm going to be fine.'

She nods, barely, her gaze fixed on the outer hall behind me. 'Just... call me when you get there.'

'Sure.'

But I don't call. I text.

And just like that, the distance between us becomes more than just miles. It becomes a strained silence. A gulf. One that I'm no longer sure we'll ever be able to cross.

6

THEO

Boat secured. *Check.*

Now for my passengers...

I turn to find Lottie doing laps around Sadie like a toddler-shaped firework – tiny, fast, and seconds from detonation.

Christ. And I'm about to put *that* on water...?

I snag a life vest from the boatman like it's body armour and intercept her mid-soar. 'Time to suit up, Captain.'

She skids to a miraculous halt and I wrestle the vest over her shoulders, zipping her in with the calm, practised ease of someone absolutely winging it.

Sadie's watching the entire thing, arms crossed, a curious twist tugging at the corner of her mouth.

I throw her a grin that says, *I've got this.*

She smiles back like she almost believes me.

And just like that, I almost believe me too.

'Ready?' I say to our captain.

'Ready!'

I help them aboard, bracing my feet as the boat rocks with their arrival. It gives me something to focus on – something that isn't the warmth of Sadie's hand in mine as she climbs in. It's a hand. Just a hand. Nothing exotic or erotic or— *Jesus*, get a grip!

I feel about as wired as Lottie looks, and I glance at Sadie. 'I think Captain might need strapping in?'

She gives an edgy laugh, pulling Lottie into her lap as she takes a seat – *thank God* – while I do the same and grab the oars.

Why did I think this was a good idea again?

Still, Lottie seems... mostly contained. Contained and chipper, which is as close to calm as you get with a three-year-old, I'm coming to realise. I row us out while she babbles non-stop about birds, boats, and everything in between, her head on a constant swivel.

And Sadie... I don't know.

She's dug out a pair of sunglasses and I can't see her eyes any more, but her head is angled to the sun, her mouth softly curved. The sight steals my breath – then my rhythm – the oars stuttering across the surface before I pull it back under control.

Her mouth twitches.

I wonder if she noticed.

Noticed and knows the cause.

Beautiful, that's what she is, that's what I want to tell her. But I can't.

I let that out and it's a slippery slope into the truth – that I want her. That I wanted her back then, too. And that's a truth neither of us can handle.

She's fresh out of a relationship from hell, seeking a new life for her and Lottie – a happy, stable life.

And me messing with that, confusing it with whatever this attraction is... it wouldn't just reopen an old wound, it would break Taylor's trust in me. Maybe even break Sadie all over again, and I can't do it. I won't.

I can make her feel better though. I hope.

'How do you feel now?'

We're in the middle of the lake. Far enough from land for the noise to fall away. Here, it's just the gentle creak of the hull, the steady lap of the water, the soft swoosh of the oars.

'Better.' She turns that tiny smile on me. 'Thank you.'

My chest eases. Just hearing her say it and knowing that she means it...

But I can't forget how she looked getting out of the car. Pale. Clammy. Flinching at every spike in sound. And I know it's him. That whatever she went through at his hand, she's still going through it now.

Because she hadn't been like this before: wary of crowds, sensitive to noise...

Sadie from her teens would have been at the heart of it.

Grinning and yelling as much as those teens we passed.

'You don't need to thank me,' I say, still rowing, still inching her away from it. 'You're doing me a favour by getting me out of the apartment too.'

Her smile lifts to one side. 'I did think you were looking a little too vampire-like.'

'Vampire-like?' I choke out.

'Sure, I'm surprised you don't shimmer in the sun like Edward Cullen.'

Now I laugh. 'Ha! Don't you be getting me mixed up in your weird Twiglet fantasies.'

She laughs too, and it's like sunshine. Real and true and there's my Sadie – no, not *my* Sadie. But the Sadie I remember. *God*, how I've *missed* her. The thought punches through me, painfully acute.

'I'd forgotten how you call it that.'

I swallow the sudden tightness in my chest.

'You say *Twilight*, I say Twiglet, same shi—'

Her brows lift above her sunnies.

'Ship!' I quickly correct.

I mouth an apology but to be fair, our captain is too engrossed in narrating a passing duck's life story to care what curse I was or wasn't about to utter. And I'm too eager to draw more of the old Sadie out... even if I am sailing too close to the wind by lumping me, her, and movie fantasies in the same breath.

Though she started it. She'd been obsessed with Edward as a teen. Edward this, Edward that. Edward Edward Edward.

Until, suddenly, she'd turned that laser focus on me...

'Mummy, what's Twiglet?'

A laugh bursts from my lips as Lottie comes to the rescue yet again. The girl deserves a full sweep of medals – gold for stopping the near-kiss in the car, silver for shutting down my thoughts, and bronze for being the ultimate third wheel.

'It's *Twilight*, not Twiglet.' Sadie shoots me a mock-scowl as she says it. 'And it's a movie Mummy used to love.'

'I like Twiglet better,' Lottie says matter of factly, and I grin as Sadie huffs, her own mouth teasing up at the corners.

'Great. And so, the corruption begins.'

'No corruption,' I say not bothering to dampen my grin, 'just an education in what constitutes a good movie versus a bad.'

'You know I'm long overdue a rewatch, and your giant flatscreen with its fancy surround sound will truly do it justice.'

'Be my guest,' I deadpan, 'so long as it's not on my watch.'

Her lips purse to the left. 'I'm sure we could find something else to watch together, if that's you offering up a movie night.'

Walked right into that one, didn't you?

And the image paints itself so clearly – a bowl of popcorn, her head tucked into my shoulder, a blanket strewn across us... cozy and domesticated and very much *not* me.

Deflection is, though...

'Captain Lottie,' I blurt out, 'fancy helping me row this mighty vessel around the island? Or are you more pirate princess than sea captain now?'

Lottie springs to her feet with a dramatic, 'ARRR!'

So much for contained.

Her tiny fist shoots skyward, narrowly missing Sadie's chin but clipping her sunglasses and sending her reeling. The boat lurches. Lottie teeters forward like a pint-sized sailor three sheets to the wind—

'Whoa. Easy there, Blackbeard!'

I lunge – one hand grabbing the straps of Lottie's life vest, the other flying out to steady Sadie before she hits the deck, or worse, the lake. The oars jam into my chest and thighs, and for one breathless second, we're a human knot of limbs, chaos, and very questionable nautical safety.

I hold us still as the boat rocks and groans back to steady.

'We good?' I ask, looking up.

Sadie lets out a breathless laugh, her sunglasses now tangled in her hair. 'That was almost the shortest voyage in history.'

Then she looks down.

To where my hand is still very much on her thigh, just beneath the frayed edge of her denim shorts.

Time stops. My pulse doesn't.

Heat rockets up my spine, awareness crackling through me. I release her like she's radioactive and drop back into my seat. My heart's hammering. From the near-capsize? Or the soft, sun-warmed skin I can still feel on my palm?

No idea. *Liar.* And I need more deflection and distraction. *Fast.*

I grip the oars with one hand and scoop Lottie into my lap with the other.

'Less jumping, more pirating, kiddo.'

And like the medal winner she is, she scrabbles for the oars with all the subtlety of a caffeinated squirrel. Distraction, personified. God love her.

I guide her small hands around the wood and lock mine beside hers.

'All right, Pirate Princess. Slow and steady wins the race. Eyes sharp for the treasure!'

I'm in full storytelling mode, which is great, because Sadie reaches behind her head to retie her hair and my brain flatlines.

Her pink tee rides up just enough to flash a sliver of midriff, and its cheerful slogan stretches right across her chest: *Sun's Out, Fun's Out.*

I swallow. *Yeah, it is.*

I try not to stare and fail heroically.

Another note to self: next time, insist everyone *wears a life vest. For safety* and *sanity.*

Then – slap! – Lottie's hands smack mine. 'Faster, Uncle Feo! Faaaaster!' She twists to glare up at me, her frown as serious as only a three-year-old can be. 'We need to find the treasure!'

I clear my throat and adjust course. 'Aye aye, Captain–Princess–*Pirate!*'

Sadie glances over, eyes hidden behind her shades again, but I bet they're full of silent laughter. Her lips certainly are.

'I just hope the treasure's worth the whiplash.'

'Oh, I've got a feeling it might be,' I murmur, doing my damnedest not to look at the curvy-cotton culprit, though that vision's seared into my retinas anyway.

Go to the park, I said. It'll be fun, I said.

Forget a life vest – I need an ejector seat and a lobotomy.

* * *

Sadie

Whoa. Did that just happen?

If not for Theo's sunglasses and the tilt of his head, I'd swear he'd been eyeing me up.

Theo. *Me.*

He couldn't have been.

Not just now. Not in the car. Not in his flat.

Just like he hadn't been seven years ago.

Because let's face it, my track record with Theo is the worst.

My track record with men, *period*, is the worst.

But the air had been charged with something – my whole body thrumming with that low-level awareness that comes from being watched.

And I *know* that sensation.

Danny did it plenty. In public, in private...

It used to thrill me.

Until he taught me to fear it.

But out here, on the boat, with my little girl and Theo – *his* eyes, *his* attention...

The only thing I'm afraid of is making a fool of myself again.

Is it any wonder I'm getting carried away, though?

The man is literally transforming before my eyes – from billionaire bachelor to babysitter of the year. Rowing a boat with my three-year-old on his lap, letting her call the shots like he's on salary and she's chairing the board.

It's ridiculous.

And unfortunately, stupidly hot.

'What's so funny?'

I lift my gaze from Lottie to find his sunglasses fixed on me, that damned grin too. A jolt of lust fires straight through my core. '*Huh?*'

'You just laughed?'

Busted.

'I did?'

He gives a low 'Mhm?' and my nipples perk up – tight, tingly, primed for more. What kind of superpower *is* that?

'*I'm not sure you want to hear it.*'

Dammit, I sound like a bloody chipmunk on helium!

'Now I definitely want to know...'

Amusement thickens his voice, and I press my thighs together, desperate to fight the ache now thrumming between them.

What the hell's wrong with me?

A bit of sun and my neglected libido is like, *Hello, Mamma!*

Don't you mean a bit of Theo?

If only.

'Sadie?'

'Yup!'

He laughs. 'That tough to admit, hey?'

Not tough. Truthful. Far too truthful. 'I'm just working out how to phrase it...'

And what to *admit*.

I chew it over, my lips shifting side to side as I take in the sight so perfect, I'm half-tempted to pull out my phone and snap a pic for posterity. But it's in Lottie's bag behind them both, and there's no way I'm risking another capsize.

Besides, I'm not entirely convinced my bra and tee are hiding the twin-peaks situation I have going on, so the more distance between us, the better.

'I'm just surprised...'

'About?'

'All this...' I gesture at Lottie and him. 'The fun, the make-believe, the way you have her wrapped around your little finger.'

He chuckles as Lottie chooses that exact moment to order a change in direction.

'Pretty sure you'll find *she's* the one with all the power here.'

'True.' I laugh. 'But you're a natural. And I'm just... surprised.'

He pulls a face. 'I think that's what they call a backhanded compliment.'

'No! It's not! Not really. I just didn't see you as the... I don't know, kid-friendly type. Or I did, but...'

His frown deepens. 'But what?'

'I just figured that all these years down the line, you'd be married with kids, and yet...' I shrug, admitting what's been bothering me since I rocked up at his swanky penthouse, afraid to set my luggage down, let alone my three-foot wrecking ball.

'*All these years...?*' He chokes out, and I bite my lips – oops. 'Why don't you just slap an OAP sticker on my arse and wheel me into the nearest care home?'

'Give over, Theo. I'm serious.'

'So am I. And I swear you've just aged me another decade or two.'

I wish. Maybe then I'd be better at switching off all the feelings he stirs up.

Then again, Theo could be fifty-five to my twenty-five and I'd still want him – much to his horror.

Because clearly, I'm a glutton for punishment.

Wanting what I can't have? Always Theo.

Wanting what's no good for me? Definitely Danny.

Possibly Theo, too.

There's no possibly about it!

And I realise my head is right. When he's this good, this kind, this incredible with Lottie – and still as off limits as ever – the risk he poses to my heart makes him 100 per cent no good for me.

But to have him in my life as a friend again...

To have him in Lottie's life – a male figure she can trust, bond with, rely on?

There's something to that. Something safe. Steady. Sure.

'You know Taylor's the same age as me, right?' he says when I don't respond.

'Yeah,' I agree softly, 'but she's living her life in reverse.'

'Meaning?'

'Meaning she spent her teens and her twenties looking after me. She never signed up for it. She just did it. Now she gets to be the party girl teenage her never got to be.'

He's quiet for a beat, his hands obeying the commands Lottie's issuing out, but his eyes are all about me. 'Is that really how you see it?'

'What?'

'Your sister's lifestyle?'

'You don't?'

'She has a good social life, sure.'

'That's one word for it.'

Irresponsible might be another but hell, who am I to judge her for having a string of lovers when I settled for one and called it so very wrong.

'Are you jealous?'

'What— no!' I blurt. 'Absolutely not. I'm happy she's out there enjoying her money and her life. Heaven knows she's worked hard for it. I just... worry.'

I trail off as my mind drifts back, uninvited, to that fight.

'Worry, what?'

I don't answer.

'Sadie?'

I inhale slowly, bracing myself, before admitting, 'I worry that she's like it because of me. That my mother set her on that path when she lumbered her with me at fifteen. And if she keeps going the way she is, she'll end up alone and unhappy. Just like Dad.' I take another breath, shake my head. 'But who am I kidding? If I'd stayed alone, I wouldn't be in this mess now.'

He holds my gaze – one strained second, two...

'But then you wouldn't have...'

He glances down and I feel his meaning all the way to the pit of my suddenly heavy stomach.

Because I wouldn't choose not to have Lottie. Not in a million years.

But I'd choose a different father for her any day of the week.

'I know.'

'Is that what you fought about?' he asks. 'Your differing opinions on relationships, on life?'

'That was a part of it.'

My eyes flit to Lottie, worrying over what she might hear, but my daughter is so deep into her Pirate Princess roleplay, she's not paying us any attention.

'She didn't approve of... *him*,' I say carefully.

Theo nods, his mouth set in a grim line, jaw flexing. I can only imagine how his eyes are behind the lenses... and it both excites and terrifies me. The passion, the anger, the care.

'From day one, she saw the signs that I refused to see. She warned me and I wouldn't listen. When I told her I was jacking in my course and moving to Ireland, you can imagine how she reacted.'

He nods again, his jaw working overtime.

'She reeled off all the reasons it was a terrible idea. And I—'

I swallow hard, my throat tightening as I remember how young, naive, and hopelessly in love I'd been. And how cruel. Driven by my misplaced love for one man, and my humiliation and... *hell*, I don't even know how to label my feelings for Theo any more. It hadn't felt like an infatuation, something born of a shitty childhood, chasing scraps, as Taylor had put it. Or 'daddy issues', as Theo had.

It had felt like so much more, because *he* was so much more. He was *still* so much more. And that's why I'm here now, trusting him to keep us safe – physically.

As for every other sense of 'safe'? I've built my walls. And they're not going anywhere.

'You?' he prompts gently. 'She said it was a bad idea, and you?'

'I accused her of being the jealous one,' I admit, the words bitter in my mouth. 'I told her she was possessive and controlling for wanting to keep me here. I dismissed everything she had done for me, threw every sacrifice she ever made for me back in her face in one stupid, careless argument.' I pause, blinking hard against the tears. 'I said a lot of stuff I wish I hadn't. I just wanted her to be happy for me. And when she wasn't... I was angry. Offended, even. Can you believe that? Offended on his behalf.'

'You couldn't have known how things would go.'

'No.'

I wrap my arms around myself, trying to contain the ache that comes with my shame, my regret... all of it sharper with the clarity only hindsight can bring.

'But I can't take back what I said.'

As for the things she said to me...

'You can apologise,' he says. 'Put it behind you.'

'I've tried. I told her I'm sorry, but...' I drag my teeth over my bottom lip, my eyes drifting to the water as I face my true fear. 'I don't know if we can ever get back to what we had. We've barely spoken since. At first, I was just too upset. Then, every time we *did* talk, she'd ask something – about him, or us – and it would spiral into another argument. Eventually, it became easier not to talk at all.'

My gaze falls to Lottie – all round cheeks, big smiles, and excited eyes. Thankfully, she takes after me in looks. Something else Danny managed to twist into a negative.

Three years, Taylor's missed out on. Three years of her niece's life that we can't get back, because I let him dictate everything.

Do I really want her to miss out on any more?

'He didn't like how close Taylor and I were,' I say automatically. 'He said it wasn't healthy. That it was some dysfunctional co-dependency that I had to cut off. And now... now I can't see a way back.'

'Of course there's a way back,' he insists. 'You're sisters, you're blood, and you love each other. There will always be a way back.'

I swallow another surge of tears. If only it were that simple.

'You just need to have a real conversation, no dancing around it; just be honest with each other and clear the air.'

'Maybe,' I murmur. 'But it's hard, you know? To get into that kind of talk when you always have to keep one eye on...'

I glance at Lottie again and he nods, saying nothing, but I sense his brain turning over, the intensity of his gaze behind his shades too. I wonder if he sees right through me. Sees my hesitation for what it is: excuses.

Because ultimately, I'm scared.

No matter how much Taylor fusses, I can't help feeling like it all comes down to guilt. Obligation, not love.

Like, after everything I put her through, she still thinks I'm her responsibility. A duty to carry, not someone to care for.

When I called and said I needed help, she came running. Of course she did.

But she didn't offer her own home as a place to crash.

She offered his. Theo's.

And if that's not a bad sign, I don't know what is.

'Why don't you go for a drink together?' Theo offers. 'And I'll watch Lottie.'

My mouth falls open. 'You're *not* serious.'

'Why not?'

Because yesterday, I was pretty sure we were *this* close to getting evicted.

Today, he's taking us out and offering to babysit.

It's too kind, too considerate, too... just way too much.

'I can't ask you to do that.'

'You're not asking, I'm offering. Besides, I owe you, Sadie. You were there for me during the worst time of my life. Or do you think I've forgotten?'

'I—'

I falter. I don't know what to think. I know how *I* feel about that time. The bond we built, or the bond I *thought* we'd built, before the kiss that broke everything. The kiss I can't forget, no matter how much I pray *he* has.

'I thought you said I was a natural at all of this.'

I wet my lips. 'I did but—'

'No buts. Just pick a night. Find out when Taylor's free and talk. No excuses, no distractions. Clear the air before it festers any more. She loves you and she only wants what's best for you.'

'So... she handed me off to you?'

The tease slips out, tangled up in the truth.

My sister, asking *her* best friend to take us in instead of offering her own home. Her best friend, who I'm half-convinced I have some kind of emotional PTSD over. The same best friend who went from accusations of *invasion* to outings in the sun, and is now offering to babysit so I can patch things up with Taylor.

Is it any wonder my heart is spinning along with my head?

'Yeah...' He grins. 'Her motives are without question. Her decision, less so.'

I give a breathy laugh. Maybe he *does* remember the kiss, after all. *Gulp.* 'On that, we can agree.'

He cocks his head, and I feel the heat of his stare behind the shades. 'Careful, Sadie,' he murmurs, 'I'll start to think you don't like living with me.'

My heart flutters. My laugh catches. 'Ha.'

If only he knew the real reason why, he'd be the one running away this time, not me.

As for meeting up with Taylor... maybe he's right. Maybe we *do* need a proper heart-to-heart.

I think back to the airport – the way Taylor held herself apart, stiff and guarded, while Lottie clung to my chest. The flicker of hurt in her eyes when she'd looked at my daughter – *her niece* – and saw, all at once, how much she'd missed out on.

Because of me. Because of what I did. What I let Danny do.

To be able to fix that. To heal it. To wrap her in a hug and tell her that I love her, that I want her in our life...

'Treasure!' Lottie shouts, her voice jarring me straight back into the present.

She's pointing furiously at a delicate, white feather floating on the water.

'We get it! Get it!'

'Aye aye, Pirate Captain!' Theo answers, dipping the oar with exaggerated care and scooping it up like some precious cargo as Lottie squeals her delight, bobbing in his lap.

I laugh at the scene they make – Lottie babbling over her treasure while Theo nods solemnly, playing along – a warmth blooming in my chest. And for a second, just a second, the weight lifts. The ache recedes. And I can almost forget everything that's brought us to this point now.

But the past never stays buried for long...

An hour later, we're back on land. The scent of sunscreen and sun-warmed grass fills the air, but the ease of the lake feels like a distant memory already. Almost like a dream. And my heart does that thing again – tightening without warning, my chest following suit.

I scan the park, eyes sweeping the shadows, hunting for something or someone I hope isn't there. But there's nothing. Just people laughing, sprawled on blankets, playing with dogs... It's one of those golden summer days when the world insists on being alive and I want to be here for it. I really do.

'We can take the picnic back home to eat,' Theo says, his eyes fixed on me – seeing everything I wish I could hide. Reading it, absorbing it, wanting to fix it.

Even though I'm not his to fix.

And I don't know what to do with that.

I'm used to a man seeing me as a problem.

But a problem worth fixing? That's new.

And somehow, it's enough to steady me. Enough to make me want to try at least.

'No,' I say, reaching for his hand without thinking. His fingers twitch in mine, his surprise as plain as my own. But I don't let go. 'We should stay.'

'You're sure?'

His thumb caresses the back of my hand, and a shiver stirs beneath my skin. Not the kind that warns. The kind that longs for more. Not that I should. Not that I can stop it either.

'Yes,' I breathe.

He gives a slow nod. 'All right. Let's try the rose garden. It's usually quieter there, and we can find some shade for this one, too.' He gestures at Lottie, who's leaning against my legs, her fingers back in her mouth, eyes wide as she takes everything in.

'Sounds perfect,' I say. Because this day, it's for Lottie as much as it is for me. Maybe even more so.

I let him lead the way and Lottie quickly slips between us again, prising our hands apart so that she can fill them with her own.

I smile. 'I think you've got a new best friend.'

He glances down at her bouncing curls, his grin making my heart take flight. 'What can I say? I'm irresistible.'

Yeah, you are...

The thought ambushes me, and I look away before he can see it on my face.

Bad track record, remember?

If only I could tattoo it across his forehead...

7

SADIE

Twenty Years Ago...

I cling to Taylor's hand as she leads me up some metal stairs. She's so big and strong and she always makes everything okay. Even when Daddy is angry. But Daddy's not here to be angry now. He's been gone for so many sleeps and my tummy *is* angry. It growls real loud and Taylor turns to smile down at me.

'Nearly there, okay?'

I nod, my mouth watering for the fish and chips she's promised. But I don't understand why we've come this way. The lady handing out food is at the front of the red-brick building and we're sneaking up the steps round back...

She raps on the peeling blue door at the top and it swings open. A boy about Taylor's age appears. Glasses shoved into his messy hair, a big smile, and eyes as green as the dino teddy clutched in my hand. I find myself smiling with him.

'Theo, this is my little sister, Mercedes. Sadie, this is my friend, Theo.'

'Hey,' he says to me, his smile softening. 'You hungry?'

I nod so much, I feel like my head's gonna fall off, and he laughs.

'Come on then.'

We head inside. The hallway is dark and gloomy, but as we pass through to the living room, everything brightens. I don't know if it's the light coming through one big window, or the food teasing at my nose, but things feel better already.

'Mum gave us a selection,' Theo says, walking up to the coffee table and grabbing a paper-wrapped package off the top of a stack. He peels it open. The hot, yummy scent building as he hands it to me. 'These are the best fish and chips in all of Hackney.'

My eyes bug out over the food mountain and Dino falls to the floor forgotten.

'Thanks, Theo,' Taylor says for me as I start tucking in as fast as I can, eyes bouncing between the food and Theo. 'She doesn't speak much.'

'Neither do I, to be fair.'

He gives me a wink and I feel my tummy flip over.

I like Theo. I like him a lot.

8

THEO

I'm not sure what's more surprising: Sadie agreeing to stay out, or the sight I make right now – sitting on a pink chequered blanket, a cucumber sandwich in one hand, a chilled beer in the other, enough food to feed an army, and a teddy bear sharing my plate.

Because *all* picnics require bears. It's a rule, apparently.

If Axel could see me now, he'd die laughing.

But he's not. And I am. Laughing, that is.

My phone's muted, work with it, and I'm all about getting Sadie to laugh with me. That is until Lottie starts squealing the park down... and not in a good way.

She bolts into Sadie's lap, her face a picture of sheer terror as she stares down an approaching pigeon. Apparently, her love of giant, white birds doesn't extend to small, grey chubsters. Go figure.

'Hey, it's okay, honey,' Sadie coos, stroking her hair. 'It's just a pigeon.'

I flick my hand out. 'Shoo!'

The pigeon barely flinches, its beady eyes locked on the crushed delight in Lottie's hand as it continues its waddling approach. There's no accounting for taste...

'What's in that thing?' I chuckle out. 'Crack?'

'Theo!' Sadie gasps, eyes laughing despite her outrage.

'Sorry, I mean... pigeon-*nip*?'

Lottie gives it a suspicious sniff. 'It's cheese!'

'Well, clearly it's very special Lottie cheese.'

She peels apart the bread to look inside, her eyes filled with wonder while Sadie shakes her head at me and smiles – and it's that smile that hits me. The one I want to see again and again.

She hasn't been the same since we got back on land. And though it's quieter here, like I hoped, she's quieter too.

And don't get me wrong, she's *trying*. But it's the obvious *need* to try that's killing me.

'All right, Lottie,' I say, ditching my sandwich and planting my beer in the grass. I wipe my hands off and get to my feet. 'I have a mission for you.'

They both blink up at me.

'A mish'un?' she slurs.

'Yup. We need someone to guard the perimeter...'

'The 'imeter?' she echoes, frowning hard.

'That's right,' I say, nodding seriously, while my brain gives me the side-eye. 'That pigeon looks mighty shifty and there could be more on the way.' I grip my hips, roll my shoulders back, and strike what I consider to be prime superhero pose. 'I need someone small, fast, and brave to fly around us for exactly thirty seconds.'

She looks at the pigeon, looks at me, the pigeon, then me...

'Do you need a demonstration?'

She nods.

Sadie's eyes go wide – *Are you seriously doing this?*

It would appear so.

You sure your *sandwich wasn't the one laced with something?*

But then, desperate times call for desperate measures...

And off I go, whirling around the roses, arms flung out like an airplane, engine hum engaged.

Oh Axel... you really would die!

The pigeon, nonplussed, backs up but stays surprisingly close.

Maybe the thing's more cuckoo than pigeon.

And you're calling the bird cuckoo; have you seen yourself?!

But it doesn't matter, because Sadie is laughing. Truly laughing. And Lottie – she's dancing on her feet, ready to join in the fun. Mission accomplished.

I stop short of the blanket, and nod to my mini recruit. 'What do you reckon, soldier? You got this?'

She's already flapping her arms. 'I can d'it!'

'Excellent... I'll hold onto this for you.' I prise the sandwich from her grasp. The last thing I want is a scene worthy of a Hitchcock movie as she's set upon by a stream of pigeons begging for the toddler-mushed delight.

'Now, GO!'

Off she races, her throaty engine sounds putting my own to shame. And Sadie lets out another chuckle, her eyes crinkling at the corners, their blue depths sparkling bright.

'That's more like it,' I say, dropping back down beside her.

'Huh?'

I smile. 'The laugh. You didn't think that ridiculous display was all for Lottie, did you?'

'Wow, am I really that bad?'

I look at her, really look. She's watching Lottie, ponytail over one shoulder, sunglasses in her hair, cheeks flushed pink... From a distance, all anyone would see is an attentive mother sitting in the shade of a tree while her daughter burns off steam. But up close, I see the way her eyes pinch with her thoughts, their depths too quick to dampen.

With a glorious day like this for a backdrop, the difference between Sadie now and Sadie pre-Danny is impossible to ignore. The T-shirt she's wearing doesn't help either. Because the fun isn't out; it's not even close.

How could someone as warm, as happy, as loving as her, ever end up trapped in a life with someone so cruel, so twisted...?

'It's not a question of being bad, it's more...' *You've changed. You're not the same light-hearted girl. You're not... happy.* I don't know how to say any of that without making her feel worse. Or dragging the past straight into the present.

But then, maybe distraction isn't the answer.

Maybe facing it head-on and talking about it is.

It's how she helped me once.

'It's more...?' she presses.

'It's him, isn't it?' I say, quietly putting the blame where it belongs. 'Your ex?'

She looks at me then, those eyes rimmed with that crushing sadness, the kind that doesn't scream – it hums. Constant and low. Like white noise she's lived with for far too long.

'Yes.'

* * *

Sadie

I draw my knees to my chest as a sudden chill washes over me. One I can't explain. Or I can, I've just never said it out loud before. Not outside of a police station, where the person didn't know me from Adam and needed it to fill in a report.

Not even with Taylor. *Especially* not with Taylor.

She knows bits, but she doesn't know it all.

Partly because I know she'll blame herself.

Partly because I know she'll blame me.

Ask me why I didn't run. Why I didn't come back sooner.

The only place I've been able to talk about it openly is online – telling my story to strangers through an anonymous blog I now run. At first, it was just an outlet, a way to feel less alone, to try and make sense of what was happening. But it became a lifeline. Not just for me, but for others too.

Now it's a full site – resources, shared stories, warning signs, chat channels... a quiet, growing community. And I'm proud of what it's become.

But that's all behind a screen, protected by anonymity.

Telling Theo, face to face?

That's different.

'It's okay, Sadie. You don't have to talk about this, not if you don't want to. But you lent me an ear when I needed it, and I can do the same for you now.'

I meet his gaze. He's stripped the hat and the shades. It's just him and those green eyes – open, steady, full of compassion.

And I want to talk.

God, I do.

But the words sit like stones in my throat.

'You can tell me anything,' he says gently. 'And I'll listen. No judgement. No fixing. Just... listen.'

I chew the corner of my mouth, eyes drifting back to the roses. To Lottie.

I believe him. It's not that I don't.

It's just that I've spent so long judging myself, I don't know how to talk about it without breaking down all over again.

Silence settles between us, but not the uncomfortable kind. Just space. Space to think. To feel. To breathe.

And then I spot a piece of my past in the garden ahead...

'I used to come here before,' I say quietly. 'I'd sit on that bench over there and vlog about the dumbest stuff – eyeshadow palettes, lipstick shades, skin-care routines.' I let out a breath, tinged with laughter and memory. 'I once reviewed a highlighter that looked like sparkly mayonnaise. Smelt like it too.'

He gives a small chuckle. 'Bold choice.'

'You could say that. In fact, I probably did.' I smile with him. 'I used to love it. Talking to the camera. Playing around with different media. Chatting with my followers.'

'I remember your YouTube channel.'

'You do?' I blink. I don't know whether to be surprised, self-conscious, or quietly touched. He was hardly my target audience.

'Yeah. You had quite a following.'

I did, but...

'You *watched* it?'

He glances away, and for a second, I swear his cheeks flush pink – unless it's just the sun catching up with him and playing tricks on me.

'I saw bits...' he says.

'Did you think I was flaunting myself too?'

'*What?*' His eyes snap back to mine. 'No.'

Of course he wouldn't. But... a soft breath slips past my lips. 'Danny did.'

I drop my gaze to the grass beside me, staring at the blades as I pluck them from the dirt – trying to hide from Theo and from the flashing images I can't escape. I stare and stare, because I won't let another tear drop. Not in Danny's name. I won't.

'He hated it. And the more successful I got, the more followers I gained, the more he hated it. Didn't matter that it brought in money. All he saw was me selling myself for attention and embarrassing him in the process.'

Theo mutters something sharp under his breath – too low for me to catch.

'That's why you shut it down, isn't it? Why it disappeared? Your channel?'

So he noticed that too... Something flickers warm and fragile in my chest as I nod.

'But by then, I'd stopped enjoying it anyway. I was always on edge, terrified he'd walk in mid-shoot and flip out, or he'd see it later and tear it apart.'

My throat tightens, the memories in free fall, my words with them.

'I figured if I just took the vlog away, took that trigger away, things would get better. Go back to how they were, when he was more loving than...' I swallow, shake my head. 'He just found other things to get angry about. The comments that used to revolve around my videos started spilling into the everyday. At first, I thought I was imagining it – the way the air shifted if I laughed too loudly, spoke too much, said something he didn't like... I kept thinking, maybe if I was quiet, if I kept myself small...' My voice thins with my breath '...then maybe he wouldn't get mad. Maybe he wouldn't break things, he wouldn't...'

...break me.

I sense Theo stiffen beside me, and I know I don't need to finish it for him to understand where it ends.

'You must think I'm a fool,' I whisper, clenching my hand in the grass. 'For staying as long as I did.'

'I don't think you're a fool,' he's quick to say. 'Not for a second. I told you – no judgement. And I meant it.'

And once again, I believe him.

But the shame, the guilt... it's still there, pressing against my ribs, urging me to explain myself.

'Maybe if he'd been physical from the start, I would've seen sense sooner. But he didn't even shout back then. He'd just ignore me. For days. Until I felt like I was disappearing. And then, right when I couldn't take it any more, he'd give me something. A little affection. Just enough to reel me back in...'

Taylor's words come back to me. How right she had been about him, about me...

While I... I'd been so wrong. So stupid. So utterly sucked in.

I rest my chin upon my knees, grip my legs tighter.

'He always knew how to make me feel like it was my fault. That he only reacted like he did because he loved me and wanted to protect me. He told me what I could wear, where I could go, who I could see, and how long for. And then...' A bitter breath slips out. 'I got pregnant.'

My eyes find Lottie, still dashing through the roses, arms stretched wide. She's chasing a butterfly now, her little-engine sound interspersed with laughter. She's loud. Free. Completely, unapologetically her.

And it guts me.

She's everything he tried to crush in me.

Which makes remembering how he reacted to her conception so much worse, my guilt swelling with it.

'I hoped things would get better. That a baby would change things. Fix things.' A chilling shiver snakes down my spine. 'But he hated that I was pregnant. And when she was born, he hated her too. Can you believe that? He said she stole my attention. That there was nothing left of me for him.'

I can't bear to look at Theo as I admit it. The shame is too thick, suffocating me as I push on...

'And the worse he got, the more I disappeared. I got so good at being quiet, I forgot how to be anything else. I couldn't leave the house without a fight, so eventually... I just didn't. I became a prisoner in my own home. Numb to everything but Lottie. She was the one thing that kept me going. And she's the reason I finally saw sense. But now...' I turn to face him, desperate to lean into what he's offering – his unspoken support, his quiet care. 'I'm tired, Theo.'

His green eyes blaze up at me, so fierce, it almost hurts to hold his stare.

'I'm so tired of feeling broken all the time.'

'You're not broken,' he says, no softness, just certainty. 'You're rebuilding. There's a difference.'

He reaches out and tucks a strand of hair behind my ear. His fingers barely graze my skin, but the warmth sinks deep into my chest, curling through the cold.

'Rebuilding?' I test the word out, my mouth woolly around it, but... 'I like it.'

'You should. Because soon enough, you'll laugh again – *really* laugh. The kind that makes you cry and your stomach ache. The kind where you snort and don't care who hears.' His lips lift slightly, and my heart skips over. 'You'll film weird videos about glittery mayonnaise, or whatever else makes you happy. You'll take off on wild adventures with Lottie, and you won't second-guess every step. You'll be *you* again, Sades.'

I huff on impulse, though I can feel it... that tiny glimmer of hope, pulling at me as I lose myself in the fire of his gaze, in the quiet conviction of his voice.

'I fear that girl's long gone.'

'Maybe. But there's nothing stopping her from coming back stronger, smarter, and more beautiful than ever.'

Beautiful?

The word knocks the air from my lungs. Of all the things he could've said...

And what did he mean by it?

Has he always thought that?

Or is he just being poetic?

Theo – *poetic*?

'I don't know how to believe that,' I say, struggling to think straight with his eyes still blazing into mine.

'Then I'll believe it for you until you can.'

Definitely, heart-stutteringly poetic.

And I want to believe him. I want to live in that version of the world, where happiness doesn't come at a cost. But...

I lick my lips and his eyes flick down. Just for a second. And that heat returns to his cheeks, twisting his fire into something else... something I refuse to see. Because I don't trust it.

While his words... they're perfect. Too perfect and dangerous with it.

Because part of me wants to reach for him again.

To use him like a Band-Aid for a wound that is mine to heal and mine alone.

'I've got you, Sadie.'

It's everything I want to hear.

And everything I'm afraid of.

Because if I let myself believe it – *really* believe it – if I let him in too far, I won't just start hoping again. I'll start feeling.

And love...

I know that path.

It only ends in pain.

'Thank you.'

My voice quivers as I tear my gaze from his and focus on Lottie. Because no matter what Theo makes me feel, one truth remains: it's me and her against the world now. And that's how it must stay.

Theo has given me a temporary haven. Nothing more, nothing less. And I'm grateful – deeply – but I need to stay focused on the end game: getting back on my feet and creating a safe, joyful home for Lottie. One that erases all trace of the one we left behind.

'Are you going to tell our pilot her thirty seconds are up, or shall I?'

He's quiet for a moment – processing what I've said, maybe second-guessing what I haven't – then he follows my gaze, lifts his bottle to his lips.

'And spoil her fun?' He smiles faintly. 'Not a chance.'

9

THEO

'I'm going to kill him.'

Hours later, having dropped Lottie and Sadie back at the penthouse, I join Axel at Royal HQ – one of Taylor's exclusive private clubs – and I'm seething. Like take a rattlesnake, step on its tail, then say 'relax' and that's where I'm at.

'Kill who?' Axel rakes a hand through his thick, black hair, dark eyes narrowing as I collapse into the leather chair opposite him and grab the whisky he slides my way. 'If this about your new assistant again, I've told you – there are easier, more legal ways to—'

'What— no!' I wince as the alcohol burns the back of my throat and wave a dismissive hand. I don't have the patience for his twisted humour. Not tonight. 'Jake's fine. He's no Jenny, but I'm cutting him slack while praying Jen will see retirement for the snooze fest it is and make a comeback.'

Axel smirks. 'Just because you live for your work doesn't mean the rest of us do.'

'I don't live for—'

He arches a lazy brow.

'Fine. Whatever. But I don't see you complaining about the money I made you.'

'I wouldn't dare. But if you're throwing about death threats, I'd like to know who, so I can decide how—'

'It's that bastard Danny. Sadie's ex.'

That wipes the smirk from his face.

He leans back – coiled muscle and quiet tension – crowding the seat built for two. 'Why the sudden fire? You already knew he was a piece of work.'

'Yeah, well, there's knowing it, and then there's hearing it from her lips and—*fuck.*'

I throw back more whisky, chasing the burn. Trying to cauterise the guilt. Trying to scorch away the nightmare she laid out in the park: her past, her twisted reality. Then comes the image I can't shake – her in Lottie's doorway before I left. Soft smile. Big eyes. Lips brushing against my cheek. Thanking me.

Thanking me for taking them out.

Thanking me for helping her see a future.

Thanking me... when I sure as hell don't deserve it.

I should've done more. When she all but disappeared from our lives, I should've known something was wrong. Should've gotten on a damn plane, found her, uncovered the truth, and brought her home.

But I didn't.

I told myself distance was better – for her, for me.

The truth was, I was a coward.

Because even then, I couldn't stop thinking about that kiss. That one reckless, stolen kiss. And it terrified me. The passion it ignited when she was too young. Too innocent. My best friend's little sister, too.

I *wanted* her. And in wanting her, I ran the other way.

Me – the supposed grown-up – letting her walk away when I should have tried to fix things. Instead, I abandoned her to that bastard. And now she's *thanking me.*

Worse than that, as her lips grazed my cheek, all I could think about was kissing her again. She was so close. So warm. So damn beautiful. Her eyes shining, her lips mere inches from mine, that delicate floral scent – hers alone – making my head spin.

And I hated myself for it.

For still wanting what I never should've wanted in the first place.

So I ran.

Again.

Before I did something completely unforgivable and totally irredeemable.

Before I betrayed Taylor's trust, and shattered Sadie's newfound faith in me.

'It's all I can do not to get on a plane to Ireland right now and—'

'And what?'

My teeth slam together, grinding away as a hundred violent images flash through my mind. None satisfying. None enough.

But each one feeds the fire under my skin.

I kept it together around Sadie and little Lottie. Kept the lid screwed on tight.

But now I'm free of them... now it's just me and the rage... and her words on repeat in my head. Of what he did – his rules, his cruelty, his control.

How long had she endured the worst before finally breaking free?

'We don't have a location for him yet,' Axel says into my silence.

'You must have some idea!'

He doesn't answer right away. Just shifts in his seat, fist flexing. Then he mutters, low and bitter: 'We've got nothing. No cards. No hotel check-ins. No digital footprint. No paper trail.' A muscle tics in his temple. 'He's ghosted.'

'Christ, if you and your team can't find him, what hope have the Garda got?'

He exhales hard through his nose. 'It's surprisingly easy to disappear when you're desperate... and smart about it.'

'Fuck. Just give me something. Anything.'

'We're watching the docks, the airports, the ferries. Every exit route in and out of the country is flagged. We've got contacts in immigration, customs, even a guy in Dublin who scrubs CCTV feeds. If he so much as shows his face, we'll know. But guys like him... they don't always bolt; they stay close, take shelter with people they trust.'

'Unless he's coming for her, then he'll have to cross the border.' I clench my jaw so tight I hear it creak. 'What's the point in a restraining order if he can just break it and vanish? What kind of justice leaves her holed up in my apartment, too scared to step outside, while he roams free?'

'You're asking the wrong man...'

I grunt. The law and Axel go way back – none of it good. He's been cuffed, cornered, questioned since he was old enough to spit back. Now he plays nice when he has to, but trust? That's long dead.

'I took her to Hyde Park today, and the difference in her once we stepped outside...' I drag a hand down my face. 'She flinched at every sound, every passer-by that got too close, her eyes darting around like some hunted animal. She used to be the life of the party, Axel. You remember? Bold, confident, funny... lighting up every room she walked into. And her followers loved that spark. Now she can't even take her kid to the swings without breaking into a cold sweat. She's terrified of her own goddamn shadow out there.'

'Give her time,' he says. 'The more she gets out, the more she'll feel in control. That fear'll ease. She just needs to feel safe again. Once she does, the rest will follow.'

'But how can she feel safe when we don't even know where he is?!'

The tattooed knuckles on one hand flash white as Axel grips his knee. He's hating this. Almost as much as I am.

'We're watching social media, too. Friends, old contacts, any account that might be tied to him or his circle. We've already flagged two burner profiles watching Sadie's public accounts. Could be him. Could be someone feeding him updates.'

'She won't post anything now. She's not stupid. Her phone, tablet, laptop – hell, even her Netflix account – are all new and untraceable.'

'Either way, we've got eyes on it. And unless he's got an endless supply of cash and places to crash, he'll have to surface eventually.'

'And when he does...' I grind out.

'And when he does,' Axel echoes, too smooth, too calm. 'We'll hand him over to the Garda. Let the system deal with him.'

'Because the system did such a bang-up job protecting her before.'

'It's what we agreed.'

'Yeah, well, I'm not feeling so law-abiding these days.'

Axel chokes on his beer and gives a rough laugh. 'Funny hearing that from you. Usually, you're the one pulling me back from the edge, but this...' He rests his pint glass on the arm of his chair, settles that cool, measured gaze on me. 'Let's stick to the plan. Drag the bastard out of hiding, haul his arse to the station. Let the law deal with him.'

'I'd rather break his face first. Then you haul him in.'

His heavy brows pull into a scowl, eyes glittering under the club lights as he runs a hand over his beard. Even without the tattoos snaking up his arms and neck, he's menacing. Meet him in a dark alley without knowing him, you'd piss yourself and run.

Hell, sometimes even *knowing* him, I want to run.

But loyalty? That's ironclad.

Deadly, but loyal as hell, thanks to the streets and the scars buried deep. Most of them were there long before I met him, back when he was fifteen. Two years older than me, but it might as well have been a decade for all he'd lived through.

Now he's as rich and free as I am, but still shackled by everything life and society threw his way. One wrong word, one wrong move – it's game over.

'This ain't you, Tanner.'

No, it isn't. But it's what her ex deserves. And it's what Axel would do. Maybe that's why his calm pisses me off even more.

I know if I asked, he'd take care of Danny. No questions. No hesitation.

But he won't endorse me handling it myself. He'd rather my hands stayed clean while he wades through the filth. Maybe it's guilt. Maybe pride. Whatever the fuck it is, I won't ask it of him. I won't let him spill blood for me. Not even Danny's.

'So it's fine for you to let loose on the bastards of this world, but I can't?'

'You're too emotionally invested.'

Emotionally invested? Too right, I am. The thought of that man laying a finger on Sadie – my God, on Lottie. She never said he did, and maybe he didn't, but...

'I want him to fucking suffer. For what he did to her. For what he did to Lottie. He hated her, you know. His own kid. Resented her for existing. Who the hell does that?'

Axel's frame tightens like a bowstring, his eyes turn to ice. *Shit.* His old man, his mum...

'Ax—'

'We'll get him,' he cuts in. 'And when we do, prison won't save him. A guy like that? Word spreads fast. Inmates don't take kindly to men who hurt women. Especially not their own kid.'

It should make me feel better.

It doesn't.

Because I've seen her face filled with fear in the daylight. I've seen the way she startles at everyday things. I've seen how tightly she holds Lottie when she thinks no one's watching.

I down the rest of my whisky and signal the waitress over. She's a tall, curvy redhead – just Axel's type. Something he's already making clear as she joins us.

I shoot him a warning glare. Taylor would kill him for hitting on her staff.

Not that he cares. He's already giving her more eye than puss-in-bloody-boots. And she's lapping it up.

What is it about a tattooed guy with black eyes?

Women lose their shit.

Add in a tortured soul?

Pure catnip.

'You're new,' he drawls out.

'Well spotted.' She flips her hair off one shoulder, scarlet-red lips lifting into a sultry smile. 'Name's Abi, and you are?'

'You can call me anything you like…'

She smirks. 'Careful, or I'll start calling you *Trouble*.'

'Only if you say it like a compliment.'

'Jesus, Axel,' I mutter. 'Taylor will have your balls.'

Abi's brows lift, amused eyes flicking between us. 'Taylor?'

'She owns the place,' I say.

'Oh!'

'Yeah.' And if she actually knew Taylor, she'd cool the come-to-bed vibe. Even when she ran the escort agency, sex with clients was never on the menu. 'We'll take the same again, thanks.'

Her gaze lingers a moment longer, then she bends to collect my empty glass. The figure-hugging, black dress – scoop neck, gold-stitched Q over one breast – doesn't leave much to the imagination. Gravity's having its way, and she's not exactly fighting it.

Which tells me she doesn't know Taylor. Or if she does, she doesn't care. Either way, she's offering exactly what Axel's after.

Me? I've only got one woman on my mind. And she's back in my penthouse, all soft-pink pyjamas and sweet smiles, wrecking me without even trying.

The waitress sashays off and I boot Axel under the table.

'And you wonder why Taylor asked me to look after Sadie instead of you,' I mutter.

'I don't wonder at all. I know what I am. You're the one who questioned it. And that says more about your conscience than mine.'

And he's not wrong.

But hearing him say it, with that all-knowing glint in his eye, lands hard. Because he *does* know – the whole sordid detail. He caught me that night, downing whisky like it could wipe her lips off mine, burn her out of my gut – much like tonight – and I cracked. Spilled everything. Desperate to purge it.

Didn't work then. Sure as hell isn't working now.

'So,' he says, dragging the word out like it tastes good. 'How's it going?'

'How's what going?'

He chuckles – low, slow, *smug*. 'Fuck. You really do have it bad.'

'You've no idea what you're talking about.'

But he does. Of course he does.

'It's not funny,' I grind out. 'My entire home's a boobytrap of plastic toys, sticky landmines and soaring toddler missiles.'

'And yet when you talk about it, your eyes light up like it's Christmas.'

I huff, shifting in my seat. 'You try it for five minutes and tell me it's not chaos.'

'I think you're protesting too much.' His smile fades, his tone dipping with it. 'Does she know about Katie?'

I stiffen. 'No. Why would I tell her about Katie?'

Axel gives a low whistle. 'You really don't see it, do you?'

'See what?'

'That maybe the reason you haven't mentioned Katie is because she's the only one who ever came close to mattering. But even Katie didn't come close enough to her.'

I laugh, but it's hollow. Forced. 'Are you really giving me insight into my love life? The guy who thinks commitment is a four-letter word.'

He doesn't even baulk. 'You were the same once. Katie was different. You kept her around longer than most. But you still didn't let her in. Why?'

I don't answer. Because honestly, I don't have one.

He leans in, brows tight, eyes burning with raw sincerity. Axel, of all people, talking *feelings*?

I blink. And just like that, my life hits a whole new level of surreal.

'It's because you've never been able to picture anyone in your life long-term... except her. Even back then. Even when you knew you couldn't have her.'

'You're reading too much into it,' I lie. 'Katie was nice, but it was never going to work. She didn't get it. She didn't get *me*. She never understood the meaning of space. And work – work always came first. It still does.'

'Maybe. Or maybe it's just easier to hide behind work than admit you've been stuck on the same girl for almost ten years.'

My gut rolls. Because no matter how 'okay' Axel makes it sound, it's not. She was eighteen to my thirty.

She's twenty-five now, though, the devil in me says.

And more vulnerable than ever, I push back.

I owe her stability and security. The kind of warmth and support she once gave me when I needed it most. When everything else went to shit, I let her see me at my worst – not Axel, not Taylor, not Mum. Just Sadie. And somehow, she managed to bring back the best.

Until that kiss.

There's nothing good about the man I was then.

Or now. Wanting what I shouldn't.

But what can I say to Axel that doesn't sound like bullshit? He knows it. I know it. So I sit in the silence until he shrugs, his voice casual again.

'Though what do I know?' He slaps his finished pint down on the table. 'Maybe you're right. Maybe you're just like me: not built for forever. Life's easier when you only have yourself to think about...'

'Yeah.' I stare at his empty glass, feeling every bit as hollow. 'Yeah, it is.'

Easier, sure.

But happier?

I thought I'd be happy when I made my first million. I was. For about five minutes. Then I wanted ten. Then a hundred. Then a billion.

I thought I was happy when I bought my first Lamborghini, my helicopter too.

I thought I was happy when I bought the penthouse in my building. The most exclusive, the most desired.

I thought I was happy when I bought my parents the holiday home we used to rent in Pembrokeshire every summer as a kid. When I paid off the mortgage on their chippy so they could run it the hours they wanted, rather than *all* the hours.

Every win, every milestone... all it ever did was make me look to the next thing.

But Sadie?

What could I ever want after her?

* * *

Sadie

I hear the soft ding of the private elevator arrive and snap my laptop shut. Don't ask me why I chose to work in the open-plan living space instead of the bedroom tonight. Maybe after our day out, I just feel like I can. Like he's truly okay with us being here. Like we're welcome even.

And it's... it's *nice*.

Being in his space. Reassuring, despite the cool, masculine tones and neat-freak vibe. I like his scent. I like his presence. I like *him*.

And I've decided that's no bad thing. So long as I keep it contained this time. No getting carried away. The fact of the matter is, I used to enjoy his company. He was as good a friend to me as he was to Taylor, before kiss-gate. Getting even a fraction of that friendship back...

Well, that'd be a win on this otherwise shitty path my life's taken.

I tune into the rustle of him shrugging off his coat, the soft thud of shoes hitting the floor, then the quiet pad of footsteps coming down the hall. My pulse quickens and I pull my plait over one shoulder, smooth down my baby-pink PJs and—

'Sadie...?'

He freezes on the threshold, one hand braced against the wall like it's the only thing keeping him upright. I'd say it's just surprise at finding me here, but his voice sounds off. Too thick. Too gruff. Too... drunk?

'Hey,' I say, easing my feet out from under me. 'Good night?'

The only light in the room comes from a single lamp I've left glowing in the corner. It messes with his green eyes, turning them near-black and glittering like glass. It sharpens his cheekbones, the stubble roughening his jaw, the crease between his brows... He looks tortured, broken.

'Theo?'

His Adam's apple bobs as he gives a stiff nod. Then he makes a sound, more grunt than word, and forks a hand through his hair. The dark-blond strands are already sticking up, like he's been tugging at them for hours. Or someone else has.

A pinch, sudden and traitorous, snags beneath my ribs.

He was with Axel, I remind myself.

Though that doesn't mean there weren't women, too.

'Is everything... okay?'

He pushes off the wall but doesn't come any closer. 'I wasn't expecting you to still be up.'

'Yeah...'

Neither was I. It's well past midnight, but my recent blog posts have triggered a wave of new followers – people reaching out for advice, support, or just someone to hear them. And I want them to feel seen, even if it means sacrificing sleep.

'...just catching up on some work.'

I slide my laptop onto the coffee table and his eyes narrow on it.

'What kind of work?'

He's never asked before. And something about the way he does now feels off. Like he's suspicious.

Or maybe I'm just projecting. A combination of guilt and Danny making everything feel pointed. But the blog is my secret. I'm not ready for anyone to know about it. Not even Taylor or Theo. Not while Danny's still out there.

'Oh, you know... admin. The odd survey.'

He nods, but his eyes stay fixed on the device like it might self-destruct at any moment. 'You're not online, are you?'

I give a small, bemused smile. 'Well, yeah, this is the twenty-first century.'

'I mean, your accounts, social media...?'

'Of course not.'

I'd have to be insane to risk that. Not after everything Taylor went through to build us a fresh start – new devices, new accounts, new everything.

A digital reset I intend to reimburse her for just as soon as I'm back on my feet.

'Good.'

I stand, and his eyes shift, catching on my bare legs with pained intent. And I swear I hear him groan. I tell myself I'm imagining it. That it's just a trick of the light, a weird burr in the music playing quietly in the background.

But as his gaze travels up my body, there's nothing imagined about the way I react – every inch of skin tingling, breath catching.

Then his eyes land on my mouth and—

Fuck.

That look. Dark. Raw. Possessive. Like he wants to taste me. Like he's imagining it now... remembering, even.

And it's not the burn of shame, I feel. Anything but.

'Theo?'

His head rocks back, eyes flaring like he's been caught... which he has. But bloody hell, I was right there with him. Against all better judgement, I was there.

He suddenly comes alive, striding for the bar in the corner of the room. 'Have you spoken to Taylor?'

The black marble bar top gleams under the accent lights that flick on as he grabs a whisky bottle off the shelf, a tumbler too – his movements stiff, urgent.

'I messaged her...' I come up behind him, cautious, but too curious to stay away. 'She's in Paris. She offered to fly back tomorrow.'

'I can do tomorrow.'

'I told her there's no rush.'

He lances me with a look. 'You need to sort this out, Sadie.'

'I know. But she's about to launch a new club out there, and you know what she's like – into every detail. I don't want to mess with her life any more than I already have.'

He sets the glass down, facing me fully, eyes blazing.

'*You're* more important than her work. No matter what happened between you two, you will always come first. You got it?'

I nod, throat dry. 'I do. But she's done so much for me already... You both have.'

A war rages in his eyes – hot, desperate... hungry. It slams into my chest, then dives lower, heat twisting through my belly. My skin prickles. My nipples tighten. A slow, traitorous throb pulses between my thighs. If he touched me now, I'd melt. If he kissed me, I'd beg.

So much for keeping it contained.

I try to take a steadying breath, but it's all him... his scent, his expensive cologne, the faint hit of whisky—

My spine stiffens, my nerves reacting to the alcohol. It's instinctual – some buried warning system. But he isn't Danny. And this isn't fear taking over.

I lick my lips and his eyes trace my tongue.

Pop.

The bottle cork jerks free in his clenched grip.

'Nightcap?' he blurts, voice tight.

'No.' I cover his glass, fingers brushing boldly against his as I step closer. 'Are you sure *you* need it?'

He looks me over, every line in his face pulled taut, pupils blown wide.

'More than you can know,' he rasps. 'Now, if you don't mind.'

He turns away, sliding the glass from under my hand, and pours – an unsteady slosh that nearly overflows.

'Go to bed, Sadie.'

My mouth quirks. 'I'm not a child. You don't get to tell me what to do.'

His eyes flutter closed as he takes a breath through his nose.

'You're right,' he grinds out. 'I'll go.'

Then he leaves – long, fast strides, whisky in hand.

'Theo?' I call out softly.

He stops cold. Shoulders squared. Back still to me.

'I told Taylor I'd see her a week on Friday. Can you have Lottie then?'

A pause. Heavy. Strained.

Then he nods. 'Of course.'

'Thanks... Sweet dreams.'

He half-laughs, half-chokes. 'Don't tempt me.'

And then he's gone. But the heat of him stays – his body, his stare, his want seared into my skin. My pulse drums hard, thighs pressed tight, breath shallow as the silence thickens.

He's not supposed to look at me like that.

And I'm not supposed to want it. Not any more.

But he did.

And I do.

God, I do.

One more second... and I'd have dragged him back just to let him burn me again.

When the hell will I learn?

10

THEO

The first thing I register is the smell – the unmistakable scent of sizzling bacon – then the noise: the distant clatter of pans, a kids' cartoon playing, and the tiny, delighted giggle that's all Lottie.

I crack open one lid and almost slam it back closed. *Whisky*.

Why did I have to hit the *whisky*?

But the answer makes my gut protest more than the hangover itself. *Sadie*.

Or rather, what *he* did to her. Danny.

And how I, the man tasked with looking after her, can't stop lusting after her.

It's fucked up. *I'm* fucked up.

I sit up slowly, the remnants of last night's drink humming behind my eyes. The smell intensifies and I don't know whether I want to race to the bathroom or the kitchen. Spew or chew. Funny. *Not*.

Holding a hand to my throbbing temple, I ease my feet to the floor. Bathroom. Then kitchen. Then... I glance at my watch. *Shit*. It's late. I'm supposed to be on with the board in an hour.

I should've set my alarm, but I haven't needed one in years. My body runs like clockwork: 6 a.m. and I'm up and at it.

But like a lot of things in my life, my body hasn't been my own since Sadie moved in. And last night, when I came home to find her on my sofa looking all—

I push the image away, but too late – it's there. Sadie. Hair in a single plait, loose wisps framing her bare, beautiful face. Her PJ top sloped off one shoulder, no bra beneath, the outline of her breasts unmissable. Shorts disappearing beneath the hem, like they were already long gone...

Blood rushes south, my cock joining the throbbing beat up top. Because *of course* that part of my anatomy would have no trouble feeling lively when the rest of me feels half-dead.

With a groan, I get up and stagger to the bathroom, step into my shower and slam it to cold. *Fuck.* I suck in a breath, my whole body recoiling as my head all but explodes, while my cock... better, much better.

It's what it deserves. What *I* deserve.

Pressing my palms to the tile, my forehead to the cool wall, I let the iced water pummel my back. I close my eyes. Try to focus on breathing.

In.

Out.

In.

Out.

Water creeps over my front, teasing the goosebumps already rising. Each rivulet a hypersensitive path that leads straight to my disobedient dick...

I shiver, but it's not the cold.

It's her.

She lingers – behind my eyes, under my ribs. Warm. Hot. Forbidden.

My hand moves before I can stop it, sliding down to wrap around my length. One tug and my head falls back, breath scraping out of me.

Yeah.

I give a slow, dragging stroke and my thighs tremble, my jaw locks.

I shouldn't be doing this. Not here. Not now. Not with Sadie—

My grip tightens, and I groan through my teeth.

Fuck.

Sadie.

The need rises, hitting harder than the headache ever did.

I see her again – last night – unfurling from my sofa like something out of a dream, another life, an alternate reality where she's mine to come home to. Bare legs, sleepy eyes, soft curves, and open arms.

But it's not last night that tips me over. That fucks me up. It's before... seven years before.

When I should have known better. Hell, maybe I did – until that kiss. One moment. One mistake. One that lit me up in places I didn't know could burn, had me clawing for what was right when all I wanted was wrong.

But now – God, if I reached for her again... how would she respond?

Would she still melt into my mouth? Would she moan like she did back then?

I pump myself harder. Faster. Slick with water. Slick with need. My stomach tightens...

What if she walked in right now? Dropped to her knees on the wet tile. Took me in hand. Mouth open and ready. Those big, blue eyes locked on mine, hungry to ruin me.

And I'd let her.

I'd fucking beg her for it.

Argh!

I come hard, muscles locking, hand still pumping as it crashes out of me. Loud. Messy. Shameful in the best fucking way.

Over a week of tension – seven years even – ripped free in one frenzied release. I brace against the wall, breath shredded, legs weak.

Wrecked.

The water keeps running. Cold. Relentless.

But inside, she burns, as hot as she ever did.

God help me.

Sadie

'Morning.'

I jump at his raspy greeting, my smile plastered on too tight. So much for playing it cool after last night's encounter...

'Morning,' I say, my eyes registering everything about him in one swift glance. The way his hair is still damp from his shower. The way his cheeks are flushed pink. The way his eyes glimmer and squint with what I'm sure is the hangover I predicted. As for his body, that pale-grey tee hugs his broad shoulders and pecs in a way that makes me want to trace every ridge, and those lounge pants... I swallow. '*Breakfast?*'

He winces, his knuckles grazing the scruff along his jaw.

Yeah, I'm back to squeaky-chipmunk mode.

'Did I fall asleep and wake up in some Stepford fantasy?'

His eyes flick to the griddle – pancakes cooking, bacon spitting – then to the towering stack already on the island, a bowl of chopped strawberries sitting pretty next to it. Picture perfect. Then his gaze slides back to me, and I forget what I'm supposed to be doing.

He pockets his hands, the fabric of his lounge pants stretching a little too much... or not enough, depending on how much you're hoping to see.

And then his question registers and hits a little too close to home. Stepford. A wife. *His.*

Heat climbs into my cheeks, and I snap back to the stove.

'Danny always said nothing beat my pancakes and crispy rashers the morning after,' I say, flipping the bacon.

It's true.

It was the one thing that cut through the worst of his mood, and gave me something to do that wasn't just waiting for him to bite. Not that Theo needs the same treatment. But I wanted to do it. And that makes all the difference.

'*Fuck*, Sadie.'

He's suddenly behind me, so close that when I turn, we're chest to chest. The only thing between us – a raised spatula and the wild thudding in my chest. His scent rises above the kitchen aroma. Clean. Fresh. Wholly him. Who needs bacon to tantalise the tastebuds when you have a Theo?

I try to catch my breath, but every inhale sends him deeper beneath my skin.

'God, I'm sorry!'

'What for?' I puff.

'I didn't think.' He drags a hand through his hair, eyes raining down on me, heavy with guilt. 'Did I remind you of him? Last night, the drink, did I—?'

Oh, God. 'You're *not* him, Theo. You could never be him.'

And yes, I'm dodging the full truth. Because sure, the drink made me think of Danny. But it didn't make me fear for my safety. Not in the way Theo's thinking.

No. What I feared most was my desire for him. And where it would take us if I gave it free rein.

'But Sades—'

'People drink, Theo. I drink. You drink. Doesn't mean we hurt people.'

'I couldn't. I would never...' His eyes burn into mine. The muscle in his jaw tics. He starts to lift a hand between us but stops, fingers curling into his palm. 'You're safe with me. You'll always be safe. I swear it.'

'I know.'

I take a breath and give him a smile, though all I want is to take that hand – now forgotten by his side – and put it on me. The only question is where. What part of me do I want him to touch the most?

It's a damned stupid question, but one my heart and head are happy to toss around as I say, 'Besides, Danny never needed a drink to hurt me. It was just the man he was. Drunk or sober, it didn't change a thing.'

Wrong thing to say. His cheeks and eyes darken, his mouth twists. 'If I ever lay eyes on that piece of—'

'Uncle Feo!'

He breaks off as Lottie comes racing between us, tablet clutched in her hands, her grin so wide and innocent and true. 'Mummy's making pancakes!'

He takes a step back, offers me a faint smile before letting it split his face in two for my daughter – hangover, be damned.

'So I see! Ain't we the lucky ones?'

Without hesitation, he swoops her into his arms, pulling an excited squeal from her little lungs.

'How about you and I set the table while Mummy works her magic here?'

He gifts me another of those smiles – private, toe-curlingly deep – then whirls away, Lottie and her cartoon-blaring tablet still in his arms. The sight is so perfect, so arresting, it takes the sharp scent of burning pancake to snap me out of it.

'Shit!'

'Mummy!' Theo calls back as Lottie peeks over his shoulder, giggling.

'Mummy just said sh—'

He presses his index finger over her lips. 'P!'

He enunciates the letter, just like he had out on the lake, and now *I'm* giggling. I can't help it. This man – the way he gets to me. Gets me, too. It's addictive, and I'm helpless to fight it.

Maybe I shouldn't even try.

Maybe I should just roll with it, knowing what it is – the present.

And what it can never be – our future.

* * *

Theo

Lottie loves getting involved.

If the grown-ups are doing it, she wants in, and laying the table is no exception. It's honestly hilarious, and I quickly learn that the safest approach is to demonstrate, then spectate... unless I fancy getting scolded.

Which, for the record, I haven't been in almost thirty years. And let me tell you, being scolded by a three-year-old? Whole new level.

Mum would have a field day witnessing this tiny dictator in action.

Actually, Mum would have a field day with this scene, full stop.

It takes twice as long, but it's totally worth it. When she's finally done – her tiny toes gripping the chair as she leans over the table to place the maple syrup down with a flourish – she beams up at me.

'Da-na! Finished!'

She straightens up at speed, and I shoot forward, hands hovering. The last thing I need is my tiny dictator face-planting off the chair, but she's surprisingly steady, all proud stance and toddler confidence.

'High five?' I say, holding up my hand.

She frowns at it. 'Five?'

'Like this.'

I gently tap her hand against mine and repeat, 'High five.'

'High five!' She grins and her legs launch into an excited jig that sees the chair wobbling and my heart goes with it.

'Easy!' I swing her down to solid ground before my fear can play out.

'Breakfast is served,' Sadie says, coming up behind us with a tray piled high, and for the umpteenth time this morning, I lose my mind.

The gym gear she's wearing is brutal... like tight, revealing, seven-year-memory-triggering brutal.

And I thought PJ-clad Sadie was bad enough. But Lycra? Fuck me, Lycra!

It should be banned in close quarters. Banned altogether, without question.

Maybe I need to enforce a dress code...

No flimsy PJs.

No short shorts.

No Lycra.

Bra MANDATORY.

Though not *this* bra.

This one squeezes her breasts together just right, and the only thing I can picture is pushing myself between them while she— Nope! I flee for the coffee before my cock fully wakes up.

'I didn't realise cooking a mammoth breakfast required marathon clothing?' I say, returning a few sanitising moments later.

She blushes up at me. 'Yeah, sorry about that.'

Hell, why is she the one apologising when you're the one perving?!

'I wasn't complaining.'

Fuck, what are you saying?!

'I mean, it's fine, you wear what you want to wear, I was just—'

You were what? Ogling her? Freaking out? Back-pedalling?

She's in the middle of loading up Lottie's plate but she stops, glances at me, blue eyes dancing, brows raised.

'I'm just going to get the syrup,' I say, doing an about-turn.

'We already have the—'

'You can never have enough!' I call back. Fuck. Fuck. Fuck. Unloading in the shower was supposed to help, but damn Jack's cocked and ready to blow.

I yank open the freezer and stand in its chilling draught. It's about as effective as the shower, but at least I'm not giving my houseguests a sodding eyeful. Literally.

'Funny place to keep the syrup...'

Her sudden proximity radiates down my back – warm, inviting... her tease more flirtatious purr than platonic fun.

You wish!

'Just grabbing ice for the juice.'

And my blue fucking balls!

She murmurs something under her breath that sounds an awful lot like, 'Good luck with that.'

'What's that?'

I glance over but she's already heading back to the table, ponytail swinging, her Lycra-sculpted cheeks giving me another injection that I unequivocally do *not* need.

My freezer joins the saint on my shoulder, pinging at me in protest.

Beep beep beep—

You beep off!

* * *

Sadie

I can't eat.

I push pancakes and strawberries around my plate while Lottie and Theo dive in. Though I get the impression Theo's eating more to keep his mouth busy than from hunger, hangover, or trying to please me.

Because I might misread his eyes, his face, even his words sometimes, but there's no mistaking what his lounge pants revealed just before he fled.

And to the freezer of all places.

The memory sends the butterflies in my stomach into overdrive. There's no way I can eat like this.

I pick up my coffee instead, eyeing him over the rim as I take a slow sip. He's concentrating *very* hard on his plate...

'I see I've got two pancake monsters in the house,' I murmur, daring him to look at me and getting a tiny thrill when he does.

'They're good,' he says around a mouthful, eyes wide, voice endearingly muffled. '*Real* good.'

He swallows – and then his eyes betray him, flicking to my chest in the swiftest glance known to man.

Hell, if I'd known gym gear would tip him over the edge, I'd have worn it sooner.

'I'm glad you approve.'

I set my coffee down and lean over to help Lottie spear another piece of pancake – purely for her benefit, of course. And I feel his gaze. The way it lingers. The way his hands tighten around his cutlery.

'I'm sorry about the Lycra at the table,' I tease, arching a brow as the devil in me calls him out. 'I was hoping to squeeze in a run on your treadmill before this one woke up, but she had other ideas, waking up at the crack of dawn...'

'The treadmill – huh?'

Now who sounds like a chipmunk...? A smile tugs at my lips.

'Still got the running bug then?'

'I wish. There hasn't been much...'

My eyes flick to Lottie, but my mind flashes to Danny. His face, his sneer: *Look at you. Desperate for attention. Parading it about.*

And then Theo. The way he looked at me. The way he's *still* looking.

Maybe Danny had a point.

The thought knocks the air out of me. Not because of Theo's reaction – no. Because of *mine*. My behaviour. God. I'm doing exactly what Danny always accused me of.

Flaunting it.

Asking for it.

My stomach twists as my face drains cold.

Slut.

The word slaps me hard – cruel, familiar.

Only his time... it's *my* voice saying it.

'Much what?'

Theo's quiet prompt tugs me back.

I blink. Shake my head as I try to shake loose the shame.

'Opportunity,' I say, my tongue too dry.

I reach for my iced juice and instantly regret it as the cubes jingle like a telltale bell.

His eyes narrow, tracking the sound. Tracking *me*. He leans back in his chair. 'You didn't fancy running with a buggy?'

'Have you seen how kids get jiggled six ways to Sunday in those things?'

He smiles, but it's small. Too small.

'A human rattle, no doubt.'

And I think that's it – that I've dodged the deeper question – when he adds, quieter now, 'He didn't like it, though. Did he?'

My throat tightens under the weight of his gaze. I can't lie. Not to him. What would be the point? He already knows enough – knows the most, even.

'No,' I admit. 'He thought my videos were attention-seeking, so you can imagine how he felt about me jogging in public. All that "showing off" in running gear...'

His hand curls into a fist beside his plate. His jaw tics, tension radiating off him like heat.

'Forget the treadmill,' he growls, voice a dark, commanding burr. 'Get outside and run, Sadie.'

I huff out a laugh. 'I don't think weaving through homicidal cyclists and double-decker buses with a buggy qualifies as cardio. It's more like an extreme sport.'

'I don't mean with Lottie.' He softens his tone, but his eyes remain tight. 'I mean on your own. When's the last time you did something *just* for you?'

I stare at him. Blank. Like the concept doesn't compute.

He tilts his head, eyes flicking to my plate. 'You've barely touched your breakfast. Why not go now? You might come back with an appetite.'

I haven't had much of an appetite in longer than I care to admit – unless you count the one I have for him. The thought alone makes my pulse skip. Dangerous. Stupid. Still true.

'But... what about Lottie?'

'What about her?' His voice is calm but firm. 'I'll watch her.'

I blink at him, thrown by the ease of it – like it's no big deal. Like *I* matter enough to be given this. A breather. A minute to myself.

'What about your work?'

'Work can wait.'

I shake my head. 'Theo... I've disrupted your life enough. I'm not messing with your schedule, too.'

'You haven't messed with anything.' His gaze doesn't waver. 'And even if you had, it's my schedule. I'll tear it up if I want to. And right now, I want you to go outside. Feel the sun on your face, the wind in your hair, and let your brain switch off.'

I swallow.

'*Go,* Sadie. Run until the only thing you hear is your own heartbeat. Think about nothing but you. Just this once.'

The urge to cry hits so hard, it's embarrassing.

'But if you're worried, I can have Axel send one of his team over, a woman to accompany you if—'

'No. No, you're right. I should do this. I *want* to. I just...' I wet my lips. 'Are you sure?'

'I'm positive.'

I turn to Lottie. 'What do you think, sweetheart? Want to play with Uncle Theo while I go for a quick run?'

She lights up like a firecracker. 'Can we hunt more treasure?'

Theo grins. 'Sure can. I was thinking...' his gaze drifts to the living area '... my sofa would actually make a great pirate ship.'

She spins on her knees to peek over the back of her chair. 'Wow, Mummy, look! Our pirate ship's cool!'

Her joy totally undoes me.

And now I really can't say no.

She's happy. She's safe. She's practically vibrating with excitement to turn Theo's apartment into the *Black Pearl,* and here I am hovering like an anxious seagull with – *with* abandonment issues.

Check that, Tay.

But then, I'm not used to this. To someone offering me a break without strings. To the idea that I can just go. For no other reason than it might make me feel good.

Danny would've called it selfish.

Hell, *I* call it selfish.

But is it? Is it really?

'Okay then.' I rise slowly. 'You be good for Uncle Theo, kiddo.'

I kiss her soft hair. She smells of strawberries and sunshine and I want to cling to it. Even though I need this. A taste of how it used it to be. How it could be again.

'There's just one condition,' Theo says, and I glance at him. 'You don't come back until you ache for all the right reasons, you hear?'

My eyebrows shoot up. *The right reasons?* I almost choke as I nod and walk. Because the only ache I've got right now is the one I get whenever a certain look comes over him, or he does things like rearrange his day just for me.

'I'm already halfway there,' I mutter under my breath, grabbing my phone and resisting the urge to kiss him goodbye too. 'Thank you.'

I'm still buzzing when I step into the elevator, nerves and anticipation fizzing through me like static. It's been years since I had a proper run – longer since I did it outside – but suddenly, I'm abuzz with the kind of energy that's got absolutely nothing to do with the impending cardio.

Then I hear his voice carry down the hall: 'Jake, hey, I'm going to need you to reschedule my ten o'clock. Yeah, the one with the board... Never mind why, just do it. Send them some of those fancy pastries from Samuel's and throw in the—'

I don't catch the rest as the doors slide closed. But the implication is loud and clear. He's not just rescheduling his day. He's rescheduling an actual freaking board meeting. Just for me.

I feel like I've stumbled into someone else's life, floating somewhere between awe and disbelief. The quiet hum of the lift cocoons me, my own private bubble, and for a second, I just stand there. Still.

This is the first time I've been in this space alone. No buggy, no Mary Poppins bag, no list of things to remember. No one to smile for, to pretend for, it's just me. *For* me.

It takes a moment to remember the security code. Another to pick the right floor to the street. I catch my reflection in the mirrored panel. Bright eyes. Flushed cheeks. Aside from the lack of sweat, I already *look* like I've been for a run.

The elevator gives a subtle jolt, the doors gliding open on the foyer. It's all polished glass and understated elegance, a bustling hive of activity too that I somehow stride right through.

'Good morning, Miss Stone,' the porter says with a nod, holding open the door.

'It really is, isn't it, Charles?' I reply, surprised by how much I mean it; my shoulders feel so light, my chest so open...

I step out into the street and for the first time in forever, I don't flinch at the world coming at me. The rush of traffic, the city noise, the commuters spilling out of coffee shops and apartment buildings. I move with it.

I don't know if it's the lasting effect of yesterday's park visit, or the growing distance from Danny, or the high of Theo wanting what's best for me, *wanting* me even – but I'm walking on air.

No, scratch that.

I'm running on it.

I dodge between pedestrians, my trainers pounding the pavement, my heart kicking like it's finally remembered what it's for. I let out a breathless laugh and a man glances up, nearly upending his fancy coffee down his equally fancy suit. I hit him with an apologetic grin and keep on going because in that moment, I realise:

I'm not scared.

I'm not hiding.

I'm not someone else's problem.

I'm *free.*

11

THEO

A week later, and Sadie's officially got her running bug back.

Every morning, she disappears off in a blur of Lycra and glowing determination, and I set up camp at the kitchen table – half-working, half-wrangling Lottie.

This morning, I'm elbow-deep in the early stages of a multi-million-pound acquisition, reviewing the financials of a failing logistics firm... while across from me, Lottie is glueing sequins to a slice of glitter-sprinkled toast.

Not paper.

Not a craft project.

Actual toast.

She hums as she works with the focused intensity of someone restoring the Sistine Chapel – head tilting side to side, pigtails twitching like antennae, bottom lip caught in her teeth. Classic concentration face. Just like her mum. And she keeps eyeing my laptop lid like it's her next canvas. Not happening.

This is my life now. And I'm not even mad about it.

So long as I remember to peel the glitter stickers off my Tom Ford shirt before today's virtual meetings, it'll be an upgrade on last Monday.

'Look, Uncle Feo! Princess Toast!'

She waves it proudly, then lunges as if she's going to eat it. I dive across the table, snatching it from her just before she bites down – nearly taking out my coffee in the process.

'I think that one's too pretty to eat,' I say. 'Try the other slice?'

She picks it up and flashes me that grin – part angel, part evil genius – and I know she's only humouring me.

Then my phone lights up beside the laptop. Jake. *Shit*. He's under strict instruction not to call before nine these Lottie-days unless the company's actively on fire.

I groan, and Lottie copies me.

It's enough to make me smile as I hit speakerphone and look for somewhere safe to stash the bedazzled toast. Possibly the bin?

'Jake, what's up?'

'Sorry to call early, boss, but Sterling's on the warpath.'

I roll my eyes, and Lottie giggles.

'He wants to speak to you.'

'I'll call him later.'

'He wants to speak to you *now*.'

Lottie stares at me, wide eyes sparkling and entranced, like I'm performing just for her. And why not? If it keeps her away from glitterfying more toast, I'm all for it.

I cross my eyes and pout. 'Well, I don't wanna talk to the big, grumpy man...'

Lottie erupts, collapsing sideways, head straight in the glitter.

'*Uh*... Mr Tanner?'

I waggle my tongue and roll my head. She has tears.

'*Theo*?'

Jake's strained use of my first name smacks me upside the head. What am I doing?

I've negotiated with oil barons. I've outbid competitors for global transport fleets. I've closed deals that could make or break empires. And my current challenge? Keeping a jam-and-glitter-stained toddler from eating sequin-glued toast like it's a Michelin-star dish.

As though to prove my point, Lottie scoops up another handful of sequins and grabs the glue-stick, her eyes flicking pointedly between me and her naked toast. I shake my head – *No!* – but she's already sprinkling like it's salt and pepper.

'Tell him I'm in serious negotiations with a tiny dictator over sequin tariffs and,' she picks up the slice, 'toast jurisdiction.'

I swoop in again, grabbing it before she takes a bite.

'Is that some kind of metaphor, or—?'

She pouts up at me. I pout back.

'Mr Tanner?'

'I'll call him.'

'Now?'

'Soon. Bye, Jake.'

I end the call, and Lottie applauds.

'Good work, Mista Tanna!' she declares, handing me the glitter-encrusted glue-stick like it's an award.

I blink at it. 'I always wanted to win an Oscar.'

She grins. 'More toast!'

'I think you've had enough toast.'

'But I want toast.'

'And I want a lot of things I can't have in life...'

Your mum being one of them.

'Called growing up, kiddo.'

That cheeky pout makes a return. And heaven help me, I'm already caving...

'Okay, okay – just one more slice.'

And that's when it hits me. Like, truly hits me.

Sadie's not the only one changing. I am.

A month ago, if someone had told me I'd be toddler-talking my way through a Monday morning, juggling a multi-million-pound deal and sequined carbs, I'd have laughed them out of the building.

And don't even get me started on the mess, the noise, and all the things I couldn't cope with when Katie was in my space.

But now?

I'm enjoying this. The chaos. The tiny feet thudding through my space. The way Lottie commandeers the sofa as her pirate ship, squealing with glee whenever she discovers stickers hidden under cushions like long-lost treasure. I don't even mind her turning my poor fern into a tiara stand. It gives the thing a quirky, lived-in kind of charm.

And Sadie...

She's lighter. Brighter. Still a little wary. Still carrying something heavy in her eyes when she thinks I'm not looking. But she's glowing more each day. Her laugh's easier. Her shoulders looser. And when she comes back from her run, hair wild, cheeks flushed and round with her smile, she looks free.

Like she's finally finding herself again.

And me?

I'm the guy up to his eyes in glitter glue and chaos, finding a side to himself he never thought possible. A side that's softer, messier, and somehow more alive.

And Axel accused me of living for my work... The man's got a nerve.

* * *

Sadie

By the time I hit the final stretch of my run, my lungs are burning – a glorious, cleansing burn that reminds me I'm alive. Still here. Still moving. Still free.

It's a wet summer's day, the sky heavy and grey, but nothing can touch this mood. Adrenaline hums in my veins. Endorphins fizz. I'm all about the rhythmic beat of my trainers hitting the pavement and the rush of being out in the world... the warm slap of the rain only adding to the sensation.

Life *is* good.

I slow as I near Theo's building, weaving through the steady morning rush – suits huddled under umbrellas, dog walkers wrangling their wet-fur monsters, gym types dripping with rain or sweat (who can tell?), and teens slouching towards the bus stop with no coats and even less enthusiasm.

And then I smell it.

Coffee.

Rich. Dark. Comforting.

Every day, I get a whiff of Theo's local independent coffee shop, Becca's Brew. And every day, I think maybe...

I know Theo keeps the good stuff at home, but there's something magical about a coffee-shop brew. A proper barista-crafted, foam-art, soul-warming cup.

Back in the pre-Danny era, it was my daily ritual: coffee and a vlog. Now, just the thought of squeezing into a cramped café sets my anxiety off. But if I can dodge traffic and puddles mid-run like some Lycra-clad ninja, surely I can handle one tiny coffee shop?

I come to a halt outside the hand-painted shop front, a vibrant rainforest scene that never fails to thrill Lottie when we pass. Heart still hammering, I peer through the steamed-up glass. It's packed. A writhing sea of bodies and a cacophony of noise.

Every instinct screams, *Pivot and go home.* But wouldn't it be nice not to return empty-handed for once? To bring Theo a treat and say, *Thank you,* and, *Hey, look what I did!*

Before I can talk myself out of it, I push inside. The noise rushes at me with the bell jangling above the door but no one so much as looks my way. Winning.

I slip into the queue behind a brunette woman who's expertly rocking a buggy with one hand while scrolling through her phone with the other. Her toddler, not much younger than Lottie, peeks out – a gorgeous afro crowning wide, rich-brown eyes that widen into fishbowls the moment they meet mine.

I smile, and he grins back, all goofy and delighted.

Okay. I've got this.

'Hey Char, you seen this?' Another woman, blonde, just ahead of her in the queue turns and hands her a colourful leaflet from a pile near the counter. 'It's a new soft play just down the road. *Finally*, we have somewhere we can run to when the weather's like this. Joshua's already climbing the walls after two days of it.'

She isn't joking. Joshua is actively trying to mount the pastry display as she speaks.

'Tell me about it,' the brunette says as her friend wrestles her kid back to her side. 'Yesterday, this one managed to spill juice all over Ian's laptop. It wasn't pretty. All this working from home is great but when Parker's having a mad half-hour or three, it's a nightmare.' She glances down at the leaflet. 'This might save my sanity as well as Ian's.'

From his vantage point in the buggy, Parker starts pointing at my trainers. 'Pink!'

I glance down, give them a twitch. 'You're right, they are.'

Parker nods, mighty pleased, and his mother turns to me.

'He's obsessed with colours right now,' she says with a smile. 'Everything is either pink, blue, or "not pink".'

I laugh lightly. 'That sounds about right.'

'You've got a little one too?' she asks.

'Yeah. Lottie. She's three.'

'Oo, have you tried this place with her?' she says, gesturing to the leaflet, and I shake my head. 'I reckon I might give it a go this afternoon. What do you reckon, Rach?'

Her friend peels her son off the serving counter. 'Definitely! You and your daughter wouldn't fancy coming too, would you?' she suddenly says to me. 'If you're free, that is...'

I blink at the invitation, startled by the warmth of it. Freaked at the ease. But maybe this is how it should be. One mum inviting another to find some calm amongst the crazy.

'My Joshua could do with meeting some girlfriends. It might rein him in a little.'

Parker's mum laughs. 'You setting Josh up on dates already, Rach?'

'*Play* dates, Char! Nothing more. No pressure, though,' she adds for my benefit. 'But we seem to be inundated with boys. Would be great to have a girl in the mix.'

I laugh again, getting swept up in their easy banter. 'I worry my Lottie would only lead him further astray.'

'Ha, I like your honesty. But let's face it, they're all a little wild at this age. Better to have them burning off steam in a place like that than destroying the home, right?'

'True,' I say, thinking about Theo's once-pristine pad. And it's tempting. Surprisingly so. Maybe I *could* do this. Maybe it's time to stop simply surviving and start shaping something new – lay down roots, build a life. A life with friends in it.

How did Theo put it?

Rebuilding.

That's what this feels like... a step towards something meaningful and mine.

'Hey, why don't we swap numbers and we can fix up a time? Here...' Joshua's mum says, pulling out her phone and handing it to me. 'Stick your details in there. My name's Rachael, this is Charlene. We live just around the corner.'

'I'm Sadie. I'm staying in the flats next door.'

'How perfect! Maybe you can talk us into running with you one day.'

Charlene laughs. 'Steady on, Rach!'

I grin as I punch in my details and hand the phone back to her.

'So you'll come?' she says.

'Yeah, I reckon so. It'll be good for Lottie to have some friends to play with.'

'You're new to the area?' Charlene asks, clearly assuming that's why my daughter doesn't have any yet.

I swallow the pang of regret and nod. 'Recently moved back.'

'Well, consider us your welcome-back crew,' Rachael says with a grin. 'It's great for the kids to have friends, but I reckon us parents need it more.'

'Amen to that,' Charlene adds. 'Mental health 101: surround yourself with other parents, people who just get it. No long explanations required, no judgement, just mutual madness.'

'Yeah...' I say automatically, chuckling along.

Not that I'd know. The last real conversation I had with another parent was back in the maternity ward, just after Lottie was born.

But if an afternoon escaping the rain at soft play means getting out of the apartment *and* giving Theo some space to work in peace, it has to be worth pushing through the nerves for.

And if it gives Lottie and me another slice of normal, then all the better.

I leave the café twenty minutes later, juggling two takeaway cups, the soft play leaflet, and a pastry box so heavy, I half-expect it to collapse in my hands. I'd love to say it's to give Theo some choice, but really, I couldn't decide. My appetite's finally woken up, and it wants to sample everything.

I snagged a cinnamon swirl, pain au chocolat, pain aux raisin, almond croissant, a bear claw for Lottie, and something extra sticky with pecans that looked so outrageously indulgent, it made me think of Theo and everything he's done for us.

Because he didn't have to make space for us. He didn't have to let Lottie take over his living room, one pirate mutiny at a time. Or spend half his Sunday flying around a rose garden just to humour us. He didn't have to turn into some pseudo-therapist, drawing me out of myself and encouraging me to live again. But he did.

And simply saying thank you will never feel enough.

When the elevator slides open, there's laughter already – Theo's voice high-pitched and ridiculous, Lottie cheering. My heart cheers with her. *This.* This is what coming home should sound like.

I step out and call, 'I come bearing gifts!'

Theo appears in the hallway, his once crisp shirt now wrinkled, a rainbow sticker on his chest, a sparkly unicorn grinning on his cheek, and somehow he's never been sexier.

It's pointless trying to deny it, so I don't.

His green eyes twinkle as they narrow on my haul. 'Did you... go to Becca's?'

I nod, my smile widening with his. 'I did.' I offer it out like the prized achievement it is. 'Carbs. And caffeine. For your valiant service.'

'My valiant service?' He slaps a hand to his chest, humour flickering into something deeper, more sincere. 'Don't you mean yours?'

We share a moment, one that tells me he knows. He sees me. Sees what this small gesture truly means.

Then Lottie barrels onto the scene. 'Mummy-Mummy! We made princess toast!'

I laugh. Really laugh. 'Maybe you don't need the extra carbs after all... or the extra juice,' I say as she rugby tackles my legs. For a second, I fear a full-on coffee-and-cake catastrophe, but Theo – ever my knight – is already there, sweeping in to take the lot.

'Yours is the coffee on my right,' I say, lifting Lottie into my arms. 'Flat white, okay?'

'Spot on,' he says, heading for the kitchen.

'*Ew*, Mummy!' Lottie wrinkles her nose and pushes away. 'You're all soggy!'

I grimace. Faced with Theo, I hadn't even thought about how I must look. I glance at the hallway mirror – blonde hair dark with rain, strands stuck to my cheeks, skin damp and flushed. *Drowned rat* just about covers it.

'I should shower,' I say, popping Lottie back on her feet. 'I feel like a soggy gym sock.'

'Nonsense,' he chuckles back. 'Come get your coffee while it's hot...'

I glance down the hall towards our quarters, but Lottie's already grabbing my hand, tugging me towards the kitchen. 'Come on, Mummy.'

'Yes, boss,' I say, letting her lead the way. What can it hurt? He's seen me now. He's also seen me looking a whole lot worse.

And speaking of things looking worse...

My gaze drifts over the living area, taking in the open books, scattered toys, and cushions tossed across the floor before settling on the kitchen table, where his work is spread out alongside Lottie's craft supplies. Glitter and toast crumbs coat the lot.

It's a mess. A genuine mess.

But the good kind of mess. The kind that shows this place is lived in.

Less museum, more home.

'What's this?'

I turn to find Theo sipping his coffee as he studies the leaflet I picked up.

'It's a new soft play area that's opened up nearby. Looks like it'll be great for Lottie. There were a couple of mums in Becca's talking about heading there this aft...' I nip my lip. 'They asked if I wanted to come along.'

'They did?' His brows arch as his eyes meet mine. 'How do you feel about that?'

I pick up my coffee, trying to act cool. 'With the weather like this, the park's a washout. So I figured, yeah, why not?' I shrug. 'Might be good for both of us.'

'Do you want me to come with you?'

I almost choke mid-sip. Theo? In a soft play centre? I can't imagine him wanting to do anything less. 'Don't be daft. You've got work. We'll be fine.'

I say it easily. Lightly. But the moment the words leave my mouth, their truth settles inside me. We *will* be fine. It *will* be fun. And it will be *us*. Just Lottie and me. As it should be. As it needs to be.

Theo has his life to return to, and we need to start building our own, even if the temptation to fold the two together is sweeter than anything on display at Becca's.

He watches me for a second longer, then smiles. 'Good. That's... good.'

* * *

Theo

Hours later, I watch the elevator doors slide closed on their cheerful chatter.

Lottie's been buzzing since she clapped eyes on the leaflet, nagging and nagging to leave. Drawn in by the bright colours, smiling kids, and the promise of adventure – all the bouncing, sliding, climbing she could ever wish for.

And beneath Sadie's nerves, I can see she's excited too. About making friends, socialising again, moving on with her life... taking real steps forward.

I told her it was good, and it is. Huge, even.

But the silence?

I glance around the kitchen, registering the little things. Sadie's lipstick-stained water glass. Lottie's sequin-studded beaker. A half-finished doodle forgotten on the table. One of Lottie's tiaras abandoned on the back of a chair. I pick it up and place it with the others on the fern, mouth twitching – part smile, part something I don't know how to name.

I *should* be thrilled. Finally, a chance to work in peace. A whole afternoon to get ahead of tomorrow's acquisition call. Time to tackle the logistics spreadsheet still mocking me from my inbox.

But instead, I'm listening.

For the stomp of tiny feet.

For Lottie's excited squeal or Sadie's exasperated shout, her quiet laugh, her storytelling lilt.

Even for that suspicious hush – the one that comes before all hell breaks loose.

Nothing.

And then I realise:

They're not just in my space any more.

They've *become* my space.

And what kind of crazy talk is that?

I'm a billionaire bachelor with a business to run, not a billionaire babysitter on endless standby.

Time to start acting like it...

At least until they get home.

* * *

Sadie

Getting lost in unfamiliar streets, nerves ticking higher with every wrong turn, my anxiety is through the roof before we even get there.

Lottie babbles from the buggy, kicking at her steamed-up rain cover, begging to get out. But I don't want her out until I know we're there. It's hard enough trying to use my phone as a sat nav without watching her wandering legs too.

I heave a sigh of relief when the building finally appears. A converted industrial unit with bold lettering in giant kid-block font standing out against the grey units all around, kind of like how Lottie's things brighten up Theo's.

The thought makes me smile past the nerves as I push through the door.

A perky teen with pigtails, looking very much like a grown-up Lottie, smiles at us from behind the vibrant welcome desk.

'Hey!' she chirps, her voice carrying over the wall of noise behind her. 'Mum and toddler, yeah?'

'Please,' I say, peeling off my rain jacket and hooking it on the buggy handle as she rings us through the system and pops the gate.

'You can park the stroller just over there...' She gestures to a buggy bay off to one side.

'Thanks.'

I steer Lottie in before unstrapping her, and she's out before I've even straightened, one arm looped around my leg as she gawps at the seemingly endless space.

It's a riot of colour and sound – neon mats, foam-covered frames, padded tunnels, gleaming ball pits, roleplay units, even a mini racetrack with toddler-sized cars zipping around. The air is thick with the tang of fresh paint, the sterile bite of disinfectant, and the bitter aroma of over-brewed coffee. Kids shriek, laugh, cry. One licks a window, several try to eat the balls, and whatever's happening in the pretend supermarket looks less Tesco, more WWE – a showdown of plastic produce and toddler wrestling.

Fun.

I peel Lottie off my leg and take her hand, but she jams the other in her mouth, making no attempt to get closer. And neither do I.

Like mother, like daughter. Two peas in a frozen pod of nerves.

'Hey, Sadie! Over here!'

I turn towards the shout and spot Rachael waving at us. She's already settled at a table beside the toddler zone – a jug of squash, cups, water bottles, and the dregs of ketchup-smeared chips in front of her. How long has she been here?

Judging by the red-faced sweat on Joshua as he clambers out of the ball pit, long enough. He waves from the edge as we join Rachael, then launches himself back in headfirst.

I give a laugh that almost sounds normal. 'Stuntman in the making.'

'Tell me about it.' She rolls her eyes. 'Hey, Lottie, I'm Rachael. Your mummy's told me all about you, and my Josh is so excited to meet you.'

Lottie leans into me but flashes a shy smile.

'Are you looking forward to having some fun?'

She nods but doesn't let go of my hand.

'Charlene's on her way,' Rachael says to me. 'She got caught up in a nappy explosion of apocalyptic proportions.'

'Oh God, I don't envy that one,' I say, trying to encourage Lottie towards the pit, but her feet have grown roots.

'Tell you what, Lottie,' Rachael says, spying my struggle. 'My Josh knows every inch of this place now. Shall I get him to show you the funnest bits?'

Lottie nods more eagerly this time, and Rachael calls him over.

He bounds up to us, bursting out, 'Hiya!'

'Josh, this is Lottie. The friend I told you about.'

Without hesitation, he turns to her, hand out. 'Wanna come on the spinny thing with me? It's cool!'

Lottie hesitates, glancing at me.

I crouch beside her. 'It's okay, baby. I'll be right here. Just wave if you need me.'

She smiles and releases my hand to grab Joshua's instead, and they toddle off towards a padded merry-go-round being spun by several sugar-fuelled toddlers. I wince, waiting for her to baulk. But she doesn't. She lets Josh help her on and giggles as they take off together.

My little girl is in.

The breath I didn't know I was holding rushes out of me.

'She always shy at first?' Rachael asks as I take a seat.

'It's her first time in a place like this,' I say, watching Lottie's face light up in real time.

Rachael lifts a brow. 'Three years without soft play? You deserve a bloody medal.'

I laugh and it's surprisingly easy. Her words simple, unweighted by our past and what we *have* survived. And it feels good. Like a clean slate. To be seen for who I am now, not where I've been.'

'Ladies!' Charlene bursts in with a giant mum bag and a theatrical sigh. 'We need to invent a nappy that can survive a toddler tsunami. We'd be billionaires.'

She flops down beside us as Parker runs ahead, joining Lottie and Joshua just as they tumble off the roundabout like mini drunks. All three dissolve into giggles – happy, tangled, and gloriously unaware of us watching on.

Conversation flows around the table... Snacks. Sleep regressions. Tantrums. Teething. It's all about the everyday, and it's everything. Not just for me, but for Lottie too.

She's finally just a kid, living her life.

And I get to be just her mum.

No fear. No past. Just this.

Extraordinary in its normality.

Perfect in its simplicity.

12

THEO

'Right... how do I look?'

I'm mid-negotiation with Lottie over the finer points of yoghurt place-ment – namely, that it doesn't belong in her hair or mine – when Sadie's voice cuts through, soft and uncertain.

I glance up, still wielding the spoon like a weapon in a dairy-based hostage situation... and completely lose my tongue.

She's standing on the threshold like something out of a Wild West daydream gone rogue. Floral dress to mid-thigh. Cute little cowboy boots. Hair curled. Eyes done. Cheeks flushed. And her lips—

God. Don't look at her lips.

Too full. Too glossy. Too...

Shit. Too late.

'That bad, hey?'

Bad?!

I want to cross the room and tell her she looks sexy as hell. Pull her in, press her tight against me, and tell her how much I want her.

Instead, I blink. Swallow. And say—

'*Yoghurt!*'

Her lips twitch. Her eyes dance. 'Pardon?'

'Uncle Feo's a frog!'

Cheers, Lottie.

'I mean, nice.' I fumble to my feet like I've forgotten the meaning of legs as well as words. 'You look nice.'

Nice. Jesus.

She arches a brow.

Even Lottie groans.

But there are no words... or none I can admit to her, anyway.

Over the past two weeks, I've seen her flushed from morning runs. I've seen her burst out of the elevator, giggling with Lottie after park trips and soft play sessions. I've seen her buzzing, sharing updates about new friends – hers *and* Lottie's – and plans for future meetups.

Every one of those moments has been a gift, and I'm grateful to have been a part of it. To see her finally living her life and basking in it.

But *this* Sadie?

The one who's had time to get ready without a toddler attached to one limb.

All dressed up for a night out...

She's something else entirely.

I try to play it cool, run a hand through my hair – and grimace when I feel the yoghurt still clinging there. 'You look a damn sight better than me, that's for sure.'

She laughs softly and steps closer, bending to grab a baby wipe from the crumpled pack by the sofa. Then she's in my space – warm, perfumed, dangerously close. She reaches up, fingers threading through my hair, and I curl mine into fists to keep them tame. I can't breathe. Can't think...

She's focused on cleaning me up, but all I can think about is making a mess of her, of me, of us.

Her perfume's dizzying. Her breath, warm against my jaw. And when she bites her lip – that soft, absent nip she does when she's nervous or concentrating – it's no longer sweet. It's lethal.

And she has no idea how hot she is. How can that be possible?

It's wrong. Fucked up. And I...

I don't care any more. She *has* to know.

'You look good, Sades,' I rasp out. '*Really* good.'

She stills, her eyes meeting mine, and I swear she sees it all.

The hunger. The torment. The fucking desperation.

Her blue depths widen, breath catching. '*Theo?*'

I take the wipe from her hand, but instead of pulling away, I lace my fingers through hers and pull her in. She comes easy, brushing up against me, and my body spasms. Every muscle coiling tight. Every nerve catching fire. Every thought narrowing down to one...

I wet my bottom lip and bow my head, catching her trembling breath as her glossy mouth parts, and—

'I did a trump!'

A triumphant raspberry explodes from hip height and we spring apart like guilty teens. Lottie!

Sadie blushes red and bites her lip, shoulders shaking with flustered laughter while I press the wipe to my face and die.

I'm not sure what's greater, the relief or the regret.

Either way, Lottie – the Queen of Timing – nails it.

And I tell myself to run with relief. Drown in the gratitude.

'It was a big one!' she crows proudly, and even I can't stop the laughter now.

'Okay, that's definitely your cue to leave.'

Sadie gives me a smile that lingers – eyes questioning, burning, wanting – even as her words shift back to business. 'Are you sure you're going to be okay with the trump monster here?'

'Absolutely,' I say, ruffling Lottie's hair – and *ugh*, more yoghurt. 'Reckon I've got a gas mask about here somewhere.'

She laughs, then tilts her head. 'And the whole bath and bed routine?'

'You mean the routine you've outlined in forensic detail?' I smirk, though my lower body's feeling anything but smug. 'Yeah, I've got this. Or don't you trust me?'

'Of course I trust you. More than trust you.' She softens. 'I'm so grateful to you, Theo. These past two weeks... they've been the best. And having your company too.'

Yeah. My company.

Breakfast. Lunch. Dinner. I've been there.

Every spare minute around work, I've made sure of it.

My theory? If getting Sadie out more has made her stronger, maybe the same could be said for me.

More exposure. Better resistance. Vaccine, anyone?

Says the guy still rocking a semi after almost kissing her – with Lottie in the room, too.

Real resilient, that.

'Maybe you should come with me tonight...'

I refocus on her, catch the way her smile fades as she says it, her hands wringing together, and it slaps the heat right out of me.

'...You and Lottie would make a good buffer.'

'Hey.' I reach for her hands, stilling them with a gentle squeeze. 'You've got this, okay? Just like you've had everything else. You'll feel better once you and Taylor have cleared the air. I promise.'

She lifts her shoulders, takes a deep breath through her nose, and nods.

'Now go.' I release her hands before my body can recharge. 'Have a good time.'

She offers a weak smile. 'I'll try.' Then she sweeps past me to kiss Lottie on the head. 'Be a good girl for Uncle Theo, kiddo. And you...' she turns to me, her smile widening into a tease '...remember who's in charge?'

I chuckle. 'That *is* me, right?'

She leaves on a cloud of perfume and laughter – a spellbinding mix that leaves me staring helplessly after her...

...until a plush cow smacks me in the face.

'Right, you.' I pluck the little missile-launcher off her chair and prop her on my hip, tickling as I go. Her giggles fill the room. 'Yoghurt war's over. Let's get you cleaned up and—'

Ping. The elevator announces its arrival. The doors slide open.

'You forget something?' I call, turning towards the hall.

'Theo, darling, I really wish you would learn to answer your phone when—'

'Mum!'

She freezes, her mouth falling open. If she wasn't already platinum grey, she would be now. Not even her bright summer dress or natural tan saves her pallor.

'I can explain.'

She shakes her head, like that'll somehow erase Lottie – and everything else about my pad that screams, *Small child lives here now.* When that doesn't work, she folds her arms, purses her lips, and gives me *that* look. The patented, world-class Mother look that sees her green eyes narrowing into a laser beam worthy of Superman.

'I'm waiting.'

* * *

Sadie

Want to know how to supercharge your anxiety?

Almost kiss the man you've wanted since forever. Then walk straight into a meeting with your estranged sister.

No pause. No real breath. Just an ache that won't quit, a belly full of nerves, and a head so loud, it feels like it could split in two as I push open the door to Taylor's Soho wine bar and—

Oh my God.

My boots hit marble – too blunt, all wrong. It's like I've stumbled off the set of *Yellowstone* and landed smack in the middle of *Suits*, and any second now, someone's going to spot my mistake and politely show me the door.

Why didn't I think to channel Taylor when I picked my outfit?

The place is so her – rich, curated, unapologetically exclusive. Deep charcoals, inky blues, warm-gold accents. Jazz floats through the air, low voices humming beneath it. Every detail, every guest, whispers money, class... legacy.

But our legacy is a council flat in Hackney with peeling walls, a pull-out bed to share, and heating by the meter. That's how far my sister's come. And I should've known better than to turn up like this.

My only saving grace? No one's looking at me except the bartender. He clocks me, disappears, and returns seconds later with...

Taylor.

My heart lifts. My stomach drops.

She walks towards me, stilettos clicking like a metronome – precise, purposeful, poised to the bone. As ever, the total opposite of me.

She looks like her mum. Dark, effortless waves. Luminous skin. Hazel eyes that see too much and give little away.

Me? I'm all mine, or so they say. Fair hair, blue eyes, a little too rough, a little too open. Dad once said I looked like a *grief-stricken fuck*. I guess that was his poetic way of remembering both our mothers.

Why my anxiety brain chose *now* to serve up that little gem, I've no idea. But as Taylor approaches, I'm reminded of everything she is, and everything she was to me.

Not just a half-sister.

But a mother.

An anchor.

My idol.

What I would've given for even a sliver of her grace and poise back then... or now.

She never needed money to look the part. But with it? She owns it. Louboutin heels. A black dress that moves like it was made for her. Salon-finish waves. Flawless make-up.

And a face I've missed more than words can say.

Yet as she nears, her pace slows. There's a quiet tension in her jaw, a flicker of hesitation in her smile.

And just like that, I see it – the nerves beneath the surface, the crack in her veneer.

Maybe we're not so different after all...

'Hi,' she says softly, stopping just a few feet away.

'Hi.'

A beat passes. Two. And then something cracks. Suddenly, her arms are around me, pulling me into a hug so fierce and fast, I don't know whether to laugh, cry, or hold on tighter. So I do all three.

'It's really good to see you,' I murmur.

'I'm so glad you asked to meet,' she says at the same time.

I pull back just enough to look up at her, and—

'Wait... are you crying?' I blink. 'You never cry.'

'Don't be ridiculous.' She waves a manicured hand in front of her face. 'I've got something in my eye.'

'In *both* eyes?'

Her mouth quivers into a smile. 'I'm allowed to be emotional.'

She sucks in a breath and leans back slightly, hands settling gently on my shoulders as her glistening hazel eyes sweep over me.

'You look amazing, Sadie. Truly. When I think of the state you were in at the airport a few weeks ago...' She shakes her head, a soft sigh escaping. 'I didn't dare touch you.'

Is she saying *that's* why she didn't hug me?

'You were so pale, clutching Lottie against you, twitching every time anyone got too close. Me included. But now, look at you. You're glowing.'

Glowing?

A flustered laugh sticks in my throat. Because any extra colour in my cheeks has less to do with healing and more to do with Theo. The way he looked at me right before I left. The way he made me feel like his every want, every need...

'This calls for champagne,' she announces.

'Champagne?' The laugh spills out.

I shouldn't be surprised. She probably drinks the good stuff for breakfast, lunch, and dinner these days. Whereas I barely drink at all.

She gestures to the bartender, who nods in silent understanding, then ushers me into a velvet booth tucked in the corner.

'What are we celebrating?' I ask.

'You breaking free of Danny, of course.'

I stare across the booth at her, eyes locking, and the guilt rises, filling my chest until I can barely breathe. 'I should've listened to you, Tay. You were trying to protect me, and I pushed you away. I hurt you. And I'm so, so sorry.'

She leans in and takes my hand, her eyes welling with mine. 'Are you *seriously* apologising to me? After I let you walk away?'

'Let me? I didn't give you a choice.'

'I had a choice. I had the means. I could've followed you. Tried harder to make you see him for the man he was.'

'And you really think I would've listened?'

She studies me quietly for a long moment. 'No, not back then. But after... I should have checked in on you. I should have flown over and seen you for myself. I should have done anything other than what I did... Nothing.'

'Why would you after everything I said? After how I was... Not calling you, not... not...' I sniff as a tear slips down my cheek, and I swipe it away. 'I'm so ashamed.'

'Hey...' She squeezes my hand. 'You were hurting. And you were protecting him. He's the bad guy in all of this, not you.'

'But I never should've said those things to you. It was cruel, unfair...'

'It wasn't *totally* unfair. There was some truth to it. You'd been my responsibility for so long that I struggled to cut the strings. I *was* overprotective. Suffocating, I believe you said.'

I flinch. 'Don't remind me.'

'But I was, Sadie. Whether it was beauty school or Danny, I didn't want you to go. And that was wrong. As for all that stuff about relationships, I'll hold my hand up to it...'

'No,' I huff. 'I had no business judging you for that.'

'It doesn't bother me.' She gives a coy smile. 'I own my sex life. I *am* all about the no-strings fun...'

I choke on a laugh. 'Okay, sis, TMI.'

Because now she's got me thinking about Theo and all the no-strings fun we could have...

I swiftly cross my legs beneath the table, squeezing them tight against the pulsing ache, too eager to wake.

'But seriously...' Her smile softens. 'If I could go back and change how we left things, I would. If I could go back and see Danny off, I'd do it in a heartbeat. But I can't. What I can do is be here for you now. For you and Lottie. I want to be a good sister. A good aunt. If you'll let me.'

I smile through the tears. 'You were always a good sister, and Lottie is the luckiest girl alive to have an aunt like you.'

She takes a shaky breath, eyes twitching to the right as the bartender approaches and she straightens up, pats my hand. 'We're definitely drinking to that.'

He pops the cork and fills our glasses discreetly before leaving us to it.

Taylor lifts her drink. 'To sisters.'

'Sisters,' I echo, clinking my glass to hers, my smile filled with love for her and the knowledge that Theo was right. No matter what life throws at us, we'll always find our way back to this, our bond that runs thicker than Dad's blood ever could.

'I'm not going to lie, though,' Taylor says with a suspiciously sly look, 'I'm a little disappointed.'

'*Disappointed?*' I cough over the champagne.

'I was hoping there was more to this meeting than going over the past.'

'More? Like what?'

'I was hoping you were going to ask to come and live with me again.'

'What?'

She shrugs. 'I didn't ask you before because I didn't want to put that pressure on you when things were so...' she licks her lips '...tenuous between us.'

'That's why you asked Theo?'

'Who else? I wanted you to be with someone I trust... someone you trusted too. I knew you'd feel safe with him, and I wanted someone to keep an eye on you. Not suffocate you, you understand. More just... be there for you.'

So many feelings race through me as she speaks – relief, understanding, love – because everything she's saying makes perfect sense... when you *don't* know about *kiss-gate*.

Her eyes narrow. 'I assume things are okay with Theo?'

'Yes. Absolutely. Theo's been great. He *is* great.'

She nods, though her eyes don't ease up. Does she doubt it? Or does she know something I don't? Or did my effusive response give too much away? Probably.

'What's wrong?' I dare to ask.

'Nothing's wrong.' She sips her fizz. 'How can anything be wrong when I have my sister back?'

I smile and take a drink.

'It's just...' she starts and my shoulders hitch, the bubbles sticking in my throat as she leans back in her seat. 'As much as I love Theo, I'm sure you're both ready to... you know.'

I frown. 'No. I don't know. Has he said something to you?'

I remember the conversation I overheard the day he took us to Hyde Park. Had there been more conversations like that? My stomach sinks. Was there more to Theo's desire for me to patch things up with Taylor? Despite how he's made me feel, what he's said, does he want me out?

'What, no?' She waves a dismissive hand, but I spy the flush creeping beneath her blusher. 'Not really.'

'*Taylor?*'

'It's more that it was a lot to ask of him, and now things are good between us, there's no reason for you not to come live with me. It would be great to spend time with Lottie and—'

'I've only just got her settled into a routine though. And I'd like to give her the summer before uprooting her again.'

'Sure. Of course.'

'But if he does want us out—'

'No, it's nothing like that. It's more that he doesn't really do living with people. He likes his space, his quiet... Like Lottie, he appreciates routine.'

I wrap an arm around my swirling stomach. 'So, he does want me out?'

'He hasn't said that, no. I just know Theo and his track record, and I'm sure it can't be easy for you living with him either. Maybe you'd relax more with me now.'

'Track record?' I give an awkward laugh. 'You say that like he's had a mum and her kid move in before...'

'God, no. He had a fiancée, though. It all went a bit sour after she moved in. I think Katie scarred him for life. Of course, it's different with you and Lottie, he'll put you up for as long as you need, but I'd understand if you were ready to move on.'

'A *fiancée*?' I say, failing to absorb the rest of my sister's ramble. Did she just say, 'put up with,' or, 'put you up' and what the actual— 'Theo was *engaged*?'

'You didn't know?'

'Why would I know?' I say, trying to sound normal and failing.

'Sorry, love. That was insensitive of me.' She frowns, misreading my reaction as being down to my absence and not the emotional hit of Theo being *that* attached to another woman. 'But yeah, they broke up about a year ago. She was nice enough, in her way. I mean, I couldn't have lived with her, but still...'

I want to laugh it all off. Say something clever. But I can't. Because the idea of him *almost* being that man to someone else... it *hurts*.

And it shouldn't. He's not mine. He never was.

And I'm so done with love. Danny's seen to that. Hell, Theo saw to it first.

But the way Theo looks at me... the way I *feel* when he's near... the chemistry, the connection... I can't deny it, and damn, maybe I shouldn't.

Maybe I need to be more like Taylor and own what I want. The fun. Take what feels good while it lasts... and leave before it ruins me all over again.

* * *

Theo

When I emerge from Lottie's room – having survived bath, book, bed – it's to find my mother grinning like the cat that got the cream *and* the mouse. Only the cream is my chilled chardonnay and the mouse... yeah, you guessed it.

'Need a top-up?'

She's standing at the floor-to-ceiling windows, glass in hand, a vibrant pop of colour against the late-evening sun. You wouldn't think she was sixty next year. Her hair's scraped up into a messy bun, her summer dress more carefree hippy than grown-up chic, and her make-up looks as natural as the golden glow to her skin.

And she's just endured the same hour I have, chasing after a racing Lottie without so much as breaking a sweat.

Wish I could say the same.

'Please, darling.'

I head to the bar, pull the bottle from the chiller and she joins me, glass outstretched. I fill it and screw the lid back on. All the while, she's watching me with open curiosity and I make a point of not meeting her eye.

'Are you not going to join me?'

I want to, but...

'I have a child in my care.'

And that's just a cop-out. The real reason I won't touch a drop is I want to be certain I have my wits about me when Sadie returns tonight. Because my God, that outfit, those boots, her body, that smile...

It'll take everything in me to resist the urge that wants to pin her to the nearest surface and claim the promise I glimpsed in her eyes.

'So you do... and it's the *best* thing I've ever witnessed!' She chuckles softly as I turn away to fill a glass with ice and water. 'You know, you should think about taking them to Pembrokeshire. A little holiday might be just what you all need.'

'We don't *need* a holiday together, Mum.' I almost drop the glass. 'I told you, they're just staying here for the summer while things blow over with her ex. That's all.'

'Yes, yes, but I don't see why you can't do that in Pembrokeshire. Your beach house is stunning, and you've hardly used it. We had so much fun there when you were little. All those summers on the beach, eating ice cream, playing in the rock pools. Lottie would love it.'

The memories choke me up, but I can't say why. Grief for Dad, grief for a future I refuse to imagine, grief for the wistful look on Mum's face.

I swallow it all down with some water, and choose my words carefully. 'Lottie isn't my kid. Sadie's not my girlfriend. This is me helping out a friend, Mum. Nothing more.'

Though she's not listening. I can tell she's already picking out a hat – a new one, not the one she chose for Katie's big day. I wince as I take another sip of water, wishing it was something stronger. But it's a good thing – for Katie as much as me – that I saw sense before we hit the aisle. I only wish I'd seen that sense sooner. Much, *much* sooner.

'Sure, sure, darling. But now she's here...'

'*Mum!*'

'Don't *Mum* me. That girl saved you from yourself after your father died. Don't think I didn't notice.'

I stare back at her – you *what*?

'Don't look so surprised. I have eyes, you know.'

Eyes that seemed forever distant back then, consumed by her grief.

'I saw you together at your father's funeral. When everyone else was at the bar, sharing stories, commiserating, I looked out the window and I saw you there in the rain. All alone. Then she came and ushered you under the trees. I saw how she spoke to you. I saw how you...'

Her throat bobs as her eyes tighten, emotion welling in her depths that I'm wholly unprepared for, while the memory floods my mind with vivid, painful clarity.

'...you broke down. With everyone else, you were strong, stoic, barely a flicker... I was so worried about you. But I didn't know how to be there for you when I was struggling to keep it together myself. But with her, you let go. I saw how she held you, how she gave you the comfort I couldn't. She was who you needed, who you trusted...'

'She was only eighteen when Dad died,' I say quietly, like it absolves me of this entire conversation.

'She was young, yes, but still an adult. She always had an older head on her shoulders. I don't know if it was her upbringing. Heaven knows it can't have been easy growing up with no mother, and a father who'd sooner look the other way than offer her any affection. But she was older than her years. Wiser. More than that, she got you to open up. To grieve. She was there for you in ways I couldn't be. In ways Taylor and Axel weren't. And I did wonder...'

'She was simply a good friend to me, and now I'm trying to be a good friend back.'

'Of course you are, darling, and your father would approve too.'

I give a tight nod, forcing the words to land somewhere I can manage them. But the grief presses in. The guilt too. All the time I missed with Dad because I was working. All those family dinners they invited me to – skipped. Because the more money I made, the less they'd have to. They could retire. Travel. Finally work to live, not live to work.

There would always be another family dinner – right?

Wrong.

And Sadie was the only one I ever poured that out to. The only one who truly understood what I'd lost – not just the future, but the past too.

And then I lost her as well.

'But forgive me for hoping that now she *is* back,' my mother says, 'things might—'

'Things might nothing, Mum. There's nothing going on between us. She's here to get back on her feet, and then she'll be gone again.'

Whatever she hears in my voice makes her brow twitch, but I don't care to find out what. I move around her, back into the living area, eyes on anything but her beady ones.

Maybe I should've shown her the door rather than the wine bottle.

She tuts softly. 'Do you honestly think I can't see that light back in your face?'

Light? What light? Unless she means the glare from the spotlight she's set on me.

'After watching you with her daughter,' she goes on, 'the way you play with her, read to her, take care of her – I'm supposed to believe that *you* really believe there's nothing more between you both?'

Of course I believe it. I have to. I'm a workaholic, just like Dad.

He did it out of necessity.

I do it by choice.

And I'll choose work every time. Work is solid. Work is controllable. Work doesn't break you. Love does. Mum taught me that.

'Theo?'

'*Yes*.' I hate the way it croaks out of me. 'Believe it.'

'Mind telling me why?'

'Because look at me! Look at my life!'

I throw a hand around the room – not the most effective gesture when the place is littered with Lottie. But it doesn't make what I'm saying any less true.

'You saw how it was with Katie. Living with someone. Sharing my space. Trying to give them what they needed while still giving work what *it* needed. It doesn't end well. Not for anyone.'

She waves a nonchalant hand. 'Katie was far too demanding and high-maintenance. The Sadie I remember—'

'That's just it,' I cut in. 'The Sadie you *remember*. She's not that girl any more. She's been through hell at the hands of her ex and now she needs stability. A chance to take her life back, on her own terms.'

'And why can't that life involve you?'

'Mum, for the love of God, will you stop?'

She stares at me hard and I stare back.

This isn't a fight she's ever going to win.

'Okay, but at least...'

'At least what?'

'At least be open to it, darling. I'd hate for you to spend the rest of your life alone.'

'Why, when it makes me happy?'

'Does it? Truly?'

I turn away, an unsteady hand raking through my hair.

'You have such wealth, Theo. More money than your father and I could ever have dreamed of, and I'm so proud of you. Your father would be proud too. But we'd see you trade it in a heartbeat for the happiness we shared.'

'The *happiness*?' I spin to face her. 'And what about the pain?'

I hate the way she blanches, her green eyes flinching at the direct hit, but...

'I know what I was like after your father passed,' she says huskily. 'And I'm sorry for it.'

'You don't need to be sorry.' I drag a hand down my face. '*I'm* sorry. I didn't say it to make you feel bad. I said it to make you stop.'

'Is that what holds you back?' she says quietly. 'Some deep-seated need to protect yourself from the pain I went through?'

I shake my head. 'I'm not held back. I tried it with Katie.'

'But Sadie isn't Katie.'

No, she isn't. And that's the real problem. Because if I were to let Sadie in, there'd be no coming back from that. And the pain if I lost her... truly lost her...

'She's Taylor's little sister.'

'And she's the woman who has you disconnected from your computer and your phone for the first time in too many years to count.'

'I'm not disconnected.'

'No? Then where's your laptop? Your phone? I can count on one hand the number of times I've seen you without one or the other. Always working, always chasing the money. But I haven't seen you check either all evening.'

'Because I'm looking after Lottie.'

'You can look after Lottie and still check your phone. And she isn't here now. Have you checked it?'

I don't even know where the damn thing is. Probably being smothered by one of Lottie's stray plushies.

'I bet you don't even know where it is,' she says, her smile triumphant, like she's just read my mind. 'The Theo I know would've had it in the back pocket of his jeans, if not already in his hand. Whether I was in the room or not.'

She's not wrong. But...

'I know you want me to settle down, Mum. Get married. Have a couple of kids. But that life – it's not for me, okay?'

She sets her wine glass down and cups my cheek.

'But it could be, darling. Don't you see?'

No, I don't dare see. Because that kind of image is as powerful as it is fragile.

I gently take her hand and lower it with a squeeze. 'Just because it's your dream doesn't make it mine too.'

You sure about that?

13

SADIE

By the time I get back to Theo's, I'm a little bit cocky and a way bit drunk, but I'm on a mission.

And that mission is Theo.

I want what eighteen-year-old me wanted, and I want it now.

And I don't care if I sound like a petulant Veruca Salt, I'm getting it.

I've been sat in Taylor's opulent surroundings all evening and we've had the most amazing, utterly cathartic night.

We've put the past to bed – and now I want to put him to bed... preferably with me on top.

I giggle as I fall out of his elevator into the softly lit hallway, his space doing more than just tickling my tummy; it tickles my nethers too.

Another giggle escapes and I press a finger to my lips, *oops,* anchoring myself to the wall as I slip out of my boots, *shh.*

I look to the left, to his quarters, and the living area just before, then to the right, to Lottie. Daughter first. Always daughter first.

It's the longest I've been without her since she was born. Surreal but true.

I pad down the hallway, extra careful to be quiet. The last thing I want to do is wake her, but...

I ease her door open. The nightlight by her bed casts a deep amber glow that barely reaches past her sleeping form. I tiptoe in, her gentle snore reaching my ears as the scent of her shampoo fills the air, and I smile. She's clutching Dino beneath her chin, just like always. Her long, dark lashes rest against her adorably pudgy cheeks, and her small smile – so much like mine this second – makes my heart bloom in my chest.

I bend to kiss her forehead and linger for a moment.

'Sleep tight, sweetheart.'

And then I hear the whisper-soft movement of the door behind me, and I know it's him. Awareness tingles along my spine as the faint aroma of freshly washed male invades my senses – has he just showered?

I straighten and turn, wanting to be in control, wanting to see him and feel the familiar burn, but have it in my grasp... I don't.

He's a dark silhouette against the glow of the hallway, his eyes like glittering obsidian locked on me. Or more specifically, my legs...

Had I given him an eyeful bending over?

Probably.

Do I care?

Not on your nelly.

Another giggle flutters up, and I move before it slips out.

He backs away as I approach, hands deep in his pockets, his jaw tightening with whatever's got him so wound up.

Me?

I hope so.

His eyes narrow as the door clicks shut behind me.

'Good time?'

His voice is a husky whisper – for Lottie's benefit, or because of me?

Either way, my nipples ping. He's like a walking remote for my body – every sound, every look, every scent.

I can only imagine what it'll be like when he touches me with intent.

Ping-ping-ping!

But I'm done imagining.

I want to know.

'The best.'

'You sort things out?'

I nod, and a tiny hiccup escapes. 'Oops!' I cover my mouth with my fingers. 'That'll be the champers!'

'Are you' – those green eyes narrow all the more – 'are you *drunk*?'

'No,' I say, shaking my head... and instantly regret it as the world gives a slow, lazy spin. I fling a hand out for balance, and find one deliciously solid pec. Yum!

My fingers flex in pure fascination, and his hand shoots around my wrist. 'Sadie...'

His low warning tone rumbles through my hand, my arm, my body... *Bullseye.*

He curses under his breath. 'Come on, I'm getting you some water and taking you to bed.'

'Is that a promise?'

He does a double take, and I grin.

He shakes his head, muttering something about my sister, I think. I can't be sure. I'm too distracted by his hand, still closed around mine, guiding me down the hall. And I instantly miss it the moment he lets go.

He grabs a glass from the kitchen cupboard, and I tear my gaze from shamelessly ogling his behind to take in the room.

Wowzers. The place is spotless. Like, seriously spotless.

Lottie's toys are stacked neatly in bins along the wall. Her books are arranged in a perfect little row on the coffee table. Her colouring paraphernalia is laid out on the kitchen island like a miniature artist's studio.

There's not a single speck of glitter in sight.

Now *that's* a miracle.

'I can't believe how tidy it is in here,' I say as he presses the glass – now filled with water – into my hand, steadying it with both of his. Double the treat. 'You put me to shame.'

'I had help.'

'Help?'

He backs away, more's the pity. And leans against the counter, arms folded, eyes watchful. Like he's unsure whether I'm going to faceplant or pounce.

And I'm not sure which he'd prefer, but I know which one I'd choose.

'My mother came.'

I snap to attention. 'Your *mother*? Did she... did she know we were here?'

'She does now.'

'Oh...' I swallow, already picturing the drama. She was always one to wear her heart on her sleeve. Kind of like someone else I know. Lil' ol' me.

It's probably one of the reasons we got on so well.

'How did she take it?'

A smile tugs at his mouth. 'Let's just say, she took great delight in watching Lottie run me ragged.'

'Oh God,' I groan. 'Was she a handful?'

'No more than usual,' he says, the obvious fondness in his eyes making my heart melt with my undies. 'Less trouble than my mother at any rate.'

I laugh softly. 'I wish I'd been here to see her.'

'She was sorry to miss you too.'

I sip my water. 'We'll have to organise something.'

'She'd like that.'

'How was Lottie with her?'

'They hit it off straight away.'

'Like mother, like son, hey?'

His smile builds, drawing my eye to the fullness of his lower lip, the well-defined cupid's bow to the top, the dark shadow of tantalising stubble shifting with the gesture...

And his smile isn't the only thing building. That dull, pulsing ache is back, stronger than ever. We might be *talking* about parents, tidiness, and toddlers, but my body's carrying on an entirely different conversation.

'So... it went well then?' His question tugs me out of my lustful stupor. 'With Taylor?'

'Yeah.' I cool my mouth off with more water, downing a swig. 'So well, she asked me to move in with her.'

'She *did*?'

I give a slow nod, trying to gauge the sudden pitch to his voice.

'What did you say?'

I hold his gaze and tell him the full truth, 'I said that Lottie and I are settled here. That it didn't feel right to uproot her again just yet.'

He stares back at me, his gaze impossible to read.

'Unless...' I hesitate, my thoughts drifting inevitably to Katie. His ex. The woman he'd loved enough to propose to... but couldn't live with. 'Unless you want us to go? I know you said we could stay for the summer, but now that you've lived with us, I'd understand if you've changed your mind. And now that Taylor's offering...'

I leave the rest hanging, breath held, heart tapping against my ribs.

His eyes stay fixed on mine, his silence stretching until I can't take it any more. 'Theo?'

'I want you to do whatever's best for you and Lottie... whatever will make you both happy.'

I bite back a curse, because of course he'd say that. It's noble. Maddening. Unbearably sweet. But two can play that game.

'And what about you, Theo? What's best for you? What will make *you* happy?'

I set my drink down harder than I mean to, and he's before me in a flash – his palm hot against my hip, like he thinks that'll steady me. But it's not my body that's off kilter. It's my heart.

I blink up at him, breath snagging in my throat as I search his eyes that give away so much and yet, not enough.

'Let's get you to bed,' he says, voice rough, hand gentle as it slides into the curve of my lower back, sending a heated shiver up my spine.

'No.' I plant my feet, forcing him to stop. 'It's not bed that I want.'

Our eyes collide, the air locked and loaded as I turn into him.

'It's you, Theo. I want *you*.'

His green eyes flare, fire catching.

'And I think you want me too.'

'*Sadie...*'

Heat pours off his tensed-up body like a furnace, and I press closer, willing it to burn.

'I'm done being the quiet one. The obedient one.' My heart thunders as I hold his gaze. 'The girl who swallows her voice and pretends her desires don't exist.' I wet my lips, and his own part in response – slow, involuntary, utterly magnetic. 'You wanted me to take my life back. This is me taking it. This is me choosing what I want.'

'This isn't what I meant,' he rasps.

I smile, just a little. 'I know. But don't look so panicked. I'm not asking you for forever. I'm asking for you – right here, right now.' Then softer, 'I'm asking you to make me forget how it was and make me see stars, because heaven knows, Danny never did.'

His jaw locks, eyes sparking with fury at the mention of Danny. But I'm not trying to manipulate him. I just need him to understand, to see what it's been like for me... and how different it could be with someone like him.

Someone kind. Considerate. Someone who would value my pleasure just as much. If not more.

'He was selfish,' I murmur, raising my hand to his chest, feeling his hot, hard heat flex beneath my touch. 'It was always about him: his needs, his gratification.' I trail my fingertips down his front. 'But you... you're not like that.' I reach the tip of his waistband. 'Are you?'

His hand clamps around my wrist, tight, trembling, his breath turning shallow.

'*Don't*, Sadie,' he warns. 'You don't know what you're asking for.'

'You're wrong. I do know.' I lean into him, my nipples straining against the confines of my bra, my thighs already slick with need. 'I'm not standing here as an eighteen-year-old virgin caught up in her first crush. I'm a woman who knows what she wants, and what she needs. And right now, that's you.'

'But I'm trying to protect *you*.'

'From what? From feeling good for once in my damn life?'

'You've been drinking.'

'So?' I roll my hips against him, catching the hard ridge of his need and relishing the soft hiss he gives. 'Seven years ago, I wanted you. Seven hours ago, I wanted you. And I want you still.' I rise up, my lips brushing his jaw, my breath warm against his skin. 'Let me prove it to you.'

'How?' It's a guttural groan.

I ease back just enough to take his hand and inch my legs apart.

'Feel...' I whisper, bunching up the hem of my dress and taking him under, pressing him to the aching, wet heart of me. A curse slips through his teeth, and I lift my eyes to his. Steady. Unashamed.

'Now tell me I don't know what I want.'

* * *

Theo

Fuck.

She's soaked.

And she's sinking my fingers in deeper like I'm the answer to her every prayer.

When I'm convinced, she's mine. I'm going to hell. It's official. But I can't take this from her. No more than I can stop my next breath.

I can control what I give her, though.

Her heavy-lidded eyes burn up at me, flickering with every pulse of pleasure coursing through her. There's a desperation in them, a shimmer of something raw and reckless as she grinds against my fingers, taking her pleasure and owning it.

All the years apart. All time either side where I looked at her and swallowed my want, told myself it wasn't right. And it's no more right now. She's still Taylor's sister. My responsibility. But then there's him. That *fucking* asshole. That cruel, selfish bastard who abused her body and crushed her spirit.

Well, fuck that. If I can do one thing, it's to obliterate his touch with my own, to rewrite everything he broke in her with care, with reverence, with every ounce of control I have left.

I fork my hand through her hair, anchor my other between her legs as she rides against me.

'I'll give you the stars, Sadie,' I grate out, 'but on one condition.'

'If this is where you tell me to ache for all the right reasons again...' she breathes, eyes glazed, body still rocking '...it's far too late for that.'

'No...' a tight laugh breaks free. 'It's not that.'

'Then what?'

She gasps as I ease the lace aside, my fingers sliding along her slick, hot seam, and it's like coming home. Pure fucking bliss. She's all heat and trembling want, so wet and so goddamn ready. I dip my fingers lower and she moans, her head falling back.

'This doesn't get to be about me,' I whisper against her, pulling back to catch her swollen clit, circling it with gentle precision as she whimpers and writhes. 'This is all about you.'

Her brow furrows in confusion, her eyes hazy with lust. 'I don't understand...'

'I'm not going to fuck you,' I murmur. 'Tonight isn't about taking anything from you.' My lips brush her temple. 'It's about giving you everything.'

Her breath stutters, then catches completely as I sink inside her. She grips my shoulder, nails biting through the cotton of my shirt as she falls back against the counter.

She's close. So fucking close already. Her hips working with wild, instinctive rhythm.

'I can feel it,' I rasp against her ear. 'Let go for me, baby.'

Her head shakes in a desperate no, even as her body says yes. 'I— I can't—'

'You can,' I whisper, pressing a kiss beneath her ear, another to her throat. 'Chase those stars.'

She moans, the sound hitching into tiny gasps.

'That's it,' I breathe. 'That's it.'

'Right there,' she pants, head thrown back, eyes wide with wonder as they lock on mine. 'Oh God, right—'

She comes hard. A full-body tremble that has her thighs clenching around my hand, her voice cracking on my name. '*Theo!*'

She clutches at my shirt, her hips jerking against me, waves crashing through her as she soaks my fingers and swallows them whole.

Fuck. I nearly lose it. I'm so fucking hard, as I hold her through it. One arm around her back, one hand still between her legs, coaxing the aftershocks as my cock strains for its own release.

But I don't move. Don't grind. Don't take an inch as I seek to undo every scar that bastard left behind.

And I'm nowhere near done.

She's too fucking beautiful like this – unravelled, empowered, free.

She collapses against me with a shaky laugh, her cheek to my chest. 'Oh my God. What was... what was the condition again?'

I lift her chin and look into her eyes, my heart beating wild in my chest as I put words to my intent. 'That you take your pleasure and feel what it's like to be worshipped...'

'I don't remember any mention of wor—'

She breaks off as I hoist her onto the counter, eyes flaring wide when I drop to my knees.

'*Theo...?*'

'Shh,' I murmur, not taking my eyes from hers as my palms glide slowly up her thighs, savouring the silken heat of her skin, the flickering fire in her glassy gaze, every tremor of anticipation her body gives me... until I reach the whisper of lace between us.

'I'm not done with you yet.'

Her breath hitches as I rip the soft pink lace from her body and slip it into my pocket.

'I don't want Lottie finding them come morning.'

She huffs out a breath. 'You think of everything.'

If she only knew 'everything' meant this moment imagined way too many times over the years. Though nothing I ever pictured comes close to the heaven before me as I spread her thighs wide. *Fuck.*

Her soft curls glisten with need, just for me.

She trembles and she whimpers. Or is that fucking me?

I lean in, lips trailing kisses along her quivering thighs, fingers parting her dripping folds to my burning gaze. Fuck, yes. I lift my eyes to hers... 'You ready?'

'Theo,' she pants, the tiniest shake of her head 'I can't. Not again, not—'

'Yes,' I growl against her, flicking my tongue over her clit. 'You can.'

Her hips buck, but I hold her down, her pleasure-filled curse shooting straight to my dick. I latch onto the swollen bud of nerves, sucking and rolling as her hands fly to my hair, her legs trembling around my shoulders, her heels digging into my back. I slide two fingers inside her, then three, four, pumping steadily as my tongue teases, tastes, devours...

'More, *fuck*, more!' she begs, so greedy, so ready, and my cock pleads with her, pre-cum seeping. Balls aching. But I refuse to give in. This is all about her. For her.

I twist my hand, tucking my thumb in and sliding deeper. Her cry comes from the very heart of her, her walls clenching around me. I can feel every flutter of muscle, every subtle shift in her body as she takes me in to the knuckle then more.

'Yes, yes— yes!' She rocks back and explodes, her pleasure flooding my mouth and my groin.

Jesus H Christ. I tense, my entire body strung tight as my cock kicks against the waistband of my trousers, desperate for relief, but I swallow it down. Her taste still on my tongue, her body still pulsing. I hold steady until she's spent. Limp, twitching, flushed.

I rise and lift her into my arms. She curls into me, her face buried into my throat, and my heart pounds within my chest. Emotions clogging up every channel within me, and I'm scared to identify a single one.

I carry her down the hall, my cock aching, my balls drawn tight. I kick open her door and one look at her bed has me freezing on the threshold.

'This is where I say goodnight.'

She blinks up at me as I set her down. 'Are you not...' she starts and I shake my head. 'But you didn't...?'

'No.' It comes out harsher than I'd like and I brush my knuckles along her cheek. 'That wasn't the deal.'

Then I turn and walk before I break it and break myself in the process.

Because it's one thing to give her pleasure when she's under my protection, but another to take it.

Yeah, you think Taylor's going to give a fuck about semantics, especially when Sadie was high on champagne too.

And do you really think it's Taylor you're worrying about?

Don't you think the problem rides a little closer to home?

Your heart, your pain, your mistake...

Fuck. Fuck. Fuck!

I rake a hand through my hair and my nostrils flare with her scent. My cock threatening to shoot its load regardless – shower, *now*.

I stride into my bedroom, strip my tee and toss my phone onto the bed. I'm entering the bathroom when the thing starts to vibrate on the sheets and my head snaps around. Who the hell would ring at this hour?

It's set to DND after midnight, and I can count on one hand the number of people who can get through that status:

Mum. Axel. Taylor. Jake.

And Jake wouldn't dare call me at this hour. Not if he still wanted his head come morning.

Which can only mean one thing.

Something's happened.

And it's bad.

I cross the room and snatch it up, half-expecting to see Taylor's name flashing up at me, ready to give me an earful for something she can't possibly know about yet.

But it's not Taylor. A chill runs down my spine as I swipe to answer.

'Axel, what is it?'

14

SADIE

I wake up hungover and happy. Any normal day, that wouldn't be possible. But today isn't normal. And the clit-pulsing, head-throbbing conflict going on in my body doesn't know whether to moan or groan.

Because no matter how much my head is cursing the second or was it the third bottle of champagne – *thank you, sis!* – my lower belly is all about the memory of what Theo did.

Actual. *Freaking.* Theo.

And it was... it was mind-blowing.

Serve-my-wildest-fantasy-on-a-platter kind of mind-blowing.

But it wasn't perfect.

Because in the cold light of day, one quiet truth remains:

He didn't kiss me.

Not once.

He made me come so hard, I didn't just see stars, I saw the whole galaxy. *Twice.* But he didn't kiss me.

And I don't know what to make of that.

But one thing's for sure, next time I take my pleasure, he's coming with me...

Because there *will* be a next time. Now that he's leapt over the moral line he drew in the sand forever ago, there's no going back.

I want as many 'take your pleasure' lessons from Theo as he's willing to give.

Don't get me wrong though, I'm not about to get all lovey-dovey. Because falling for Theo all over again, only to be rejected all over again, would be a sorry end to an even sorrier tale. And I'm sick of being sorry.

I'm taking all the good I can squeeze out of this new lease of life – and my temporary one with Theo – and moving forward.

Danny's still out there, I know. But I've quit letting him control me from afar, and it feels damn good.

I roll over in bed, a slow smile spreading... then do a double take. There's a fresh glass of water on the nightstand, a bottle of electrolytes, and a strip of painkillers. All accompanied by a note. I reach out, fingers unsteady as I pick it up:

Just in case, T x

My smile grows even as my head protests the sudden surge of warmth.
Theo, Theo, Theo...

I pop two pills and take a sip of water. Tap my phone awake and almost back up. *9 a.m.!*

Lottie never sleeps past six. *Ever.*

I throw off the duvet and launch upright. *Ow,* big mistake. I grip my throbbing temple and the mattress edge. Take a shallow breath and try not to die. Then I...

Sta-nd...

Put one foot in front of the o-other...

And open the door, ears straining for signs of life.

But there's no thundering of feet, no clatter of toys, no raised voices. Just the distant hum of the TV and the soft burr of Theo's voice. I pad towards it and find him cosied up with Lottie on the sofa, Kids TV on the box, though neither of them are watching. They're both absorbed in her favourite dino book.

Okay, okay, okay.

Heart, give over.

Ovaries, too.

It *is* one of the sweetest sights I've ever seen – but not one to get all goo-goo-eyed over.

It's all about the fun, remember.

Not, future family or forever.

Just fun!

And what fun last night was...

The memory sends my cheeks blazing – because yes, I asked for it, and yes, he delivered – but without the confidence-boosting champers in my system, I'm not feeling quite so cocky now.

Plus, I must look like hell.

Last night, the bubbles made me feel like Beyoncé.

This morning?

Like a gremlin who ate after midnight.

I fork my hand through my hair and it gets stuck in my day-old curls – ugh!

What was I thinking, leaving my room without glancing in a mirror?

I briefly consider tiptoeing back, but then his head turns and—

'Morning!' I blurt, tugging the hand from my hair to raise it in a self-conscious wave while the other pulls on the hem of the Guns N' Roses tee I threw on before bed.

'Mummy!' Lottie grins, her bunny-slippered feet kicking, though she doesn't budge from Theo's side. And really, who can blame her? If I had Theo's arm wrapped around me, I wouldn't move either.

Dangerous, dangerous thoughts.

'Hey,' Theo says softly, his eyes full of sympathy for my self-inflicted pain.

And to my horror, I get the weirdest urge to cry.

Ridiculous, I know. But compassion... for my hangover?

Danny would've laughed. Maybe tossed me a paracetamol like a dog treat – after I'd nursed *his* hangovers with pancakes and bacon and no complaint.

Or am I misreading Theo entirely?

Mistaking guilt for compassion in that overly warm gaze?

Is he worrying over what we did – what *I* demanded and he delivered?

I replay it all – every word, every touch, every feeling – and it shoots straight to my pulse, the throbbing ache almost as acute as the banging in my skull.

'You okay?' he says, his intent gaze stripping me bare.

'Yeah.' I grin too hard, too bright, desperate to show him I'm good. Because last night wasn't just good. It was *everything*. 'Thanks for the meds.'

'You're welcome.'

His gaze dips to the hem of my tee, lingers, then lifts – darker, hotter. His throat shifts. Maybe I'm not the only one reliving last night...

Then I remember how I *look* and—

'Is there coffee?' I ask weakly.

He nods, and I scarper with a swift, 'Great. Thanks.'

Coffee. Then shower. Then humanity once more.

'I'm just going to speak to your mum a second...'

Oh no. Something in his tone to Lottie makes my stomach flip.

Is this it? The part where he tells me it was a mistake? That he's sorry?

I'm nowhere near human enough to survive that.

Especially not while we're standing in the exact spot where he... *gulp*.

I grab the biggest mug I can find and tug the coffee off the hotplate. My ears tingle as his footsteps approach. My spine too.

'You sure you're okay?'

He's so close, I can feel his heat through my tee, his cologne threading through the steam rising off the coffee as I pour. It's a heady mix that sends my lashes closing as I breathe in deeper.

'Sadie?'

'100 per cent!' I chirp, plonking the carafe back. 'Or I will be once these meds kick in and I've showered.'

I skirt around him to the fridge, letting my hair fall like a shield around my puffy face, but when I swing the door shut, he's right there. Close. Brooding.

'Jesus, Theo!' I blurt, heart thudding.

'Steady,' he murmurs, catching my arm. His grip warm, gentle, sure. God, he looks good. Like, Coca-Cola advert, mouth-wateringly good. White tee, blue jeans, smelling of heaven... or sin, depending on where your head wants to go.

And me? I'm a walking ad for how *not* to look after being gifted the best two orgasms of your life.

It probably wasn't desire darkening his gaze.

More likely regret – the kind that follows clarity, daylight... and a gremlin sighting.

'Promise me you're okay.'

I force myself to meet his gaze and nod. Though the intensity in his eyes, the tightness at their corners... it isn't me I'm worried about. 'Are you?'

'This isn't about how I feel. It's about how *you* feel. I thought I made that clear.'

My heart stumbles. He did. Abundantly. Twice.

And now, the way he says it – low, certain, fervent with care – it hits me in the chest, the stomach... lower.

Then his thumb starts to circle over my skin – dizzying, distracting, delectably divine...

'Sadie?'

'I promise you, I'm fine.' I breathe. 'More than fine...'

I lick my lips, and his eyes track the motion. His thumb stills. His mouth parts – an invitation or an impulse? Either way, I'm hooked and ready to plunder.

If I'd thought to brush my teeth, that is. Bugger.

'Thank you,' I say instead.

'*Thank you*?' he echoes, brow furrowing.

'For last night.'

'You don't need to thank me...' He drags in a breath, his eyes lingering on my lips and then he's stepping back, his eyes snapping up. 'But I do need you to pack.'

'*What*?' My gut crashes down on the low-burning heat, snuffing it out cold. I close the distance he created, glance at Lottie – still engrossed in her cartoon – and lower my voice. 'You want us *out*? I know last night was—'

'No,' he cuts in, hand raking through his hair as he puts the centre island between us. 'This has nothing to do with what happened last night... unless you count the idea Mum put in my head.'

The flicker of a smile crosses his lips, but it doesn't touch his eyes. And it's those green depths that have me teetering on the edge of all-out panic.

'What idea?' I ask, setting the milk down before I drop it and clutching my head.

'To take you and Lottie away.'

'*Away*?'

He nods.

'*Where*?'

'Pembrokeshire.'

I blink, hand flying to the counter before I fall on it. 'You want to take me and Lottie... *to Pembrokeshire*?'

'Yes. Today.'

'*Today*?' I gawp.

Either my hangover is scrambling the words coming out of his mouth, or this really is as mad as it sounds.

'What am I missing?'

'Nothing.' He shrugs as he looks away. I can't tell if he's looking at Lottie or past her, but I get the impression he's just not looking at me.

And can you blame him, Ms Gremlin?

'I loved my summers there as a kid. And I think you'd love it too.'

'I'm sure I would, but—'

'Look, I know you said Lottie's settled here, but she'd get so much more out of being there. Having the beach on her doorstep, rock pools to explore, woodland trails, too. Real space to just... be a kid.'

Yeah, it sounds idyllic. But it's so left field. And why the sudden urgency?

'What about your work?'

'I can work just as easily from my place there. It's remote but not *that* remote.'

'I was going to meet the girls at the coffee shop this afternoon, maybe we could—'

His jaw twitches. 'It's better for me if we set off this morning.'

'Right, this morning...' I drawl, nodding slowly, still convinced I'm missing something. I just can't work out if it's a *good* thing, or a bad.

'It'll be a holiday for you both, Sadie.' His eyes come back to me, his tone shifting into something softer, more persuasive. 'You and Lottie deserve that after everything you've been through. I should've thought of it sooner, but now I have, let me do this for you. For both of you. Please.'

And here come the tears again...

Because Lottie and I have never had a holiday together. Not one. Unless you count the room above the pub Danny booked for a friend's wedding. And even then, it was to squirrel us away while he drank the night away with his mates. Close enough to keep an eye on, but not too close.

And this is Theo – *workaholic* Theo – with his ordered life and meticulous routines, the same ones we've been derailing ever since we got here, now offering to take us away and derail it even more.

But for the first time since arriving, I don't feel bad about it.

Not if it means he's going to take a long-overdue holiday too...

'We go on one condition,' I say.

His mouth lifts to one side, eyes sparkling. 'You're setting the conditions now?'

I cross my arms. 'I think it's my turn.'

'Name it.'

'You take some time off too.'

'Deal.'

No hesitation. No qualifiers. Just that.

My arms fall to my sides, body going slack with surprise.

'Really?'

'Really.'

Then he runs a hand through his hair again, and I'm struck by the memory of doing the same – fingers tugging, twisting, nails raking...

'Stop overthinking it, Sadie. And get packing.'

'You really are serious?'

He grins, but there's still tension around his eyes – a heaviness I can't quite place.

'Have you ever known me to be anything else?'

I think about how serious he'd been last night when he told me I could come again. And mentally relive the highlight: me, spread wide on his kitchen counter, reaching for the stars he promised...

...and claiming every single one.

* * *

Theo

I watch Sadie walk away, fingers clasped tight behind my head, every muscle taut with the urge to chase after her.

She came undone on me just hours ago – shaking, gasping my name, body giving me everything. Trusting me. And fuck, I want her. So badly, it burns.

But that burn is nothing compared to the truth I'm holding back.

Because while I was making her see stars, *he* was out there. That bastard Danny. He slipped under everyone's radar and cornered Taylor outside her building. Left her shaken but she walked away unharmed. Thank God.

Sadie wouldn't have been so lucky.

And that's what guts me.

Because she's finally dragging herself out of the wreckage he left – laughing again, pushing boundaries, owning her pleasure... She's shining. Coming back to life in front of me. And he came *this* close to destroying it all. He *is* this close to destroying it all.

Because the moment Sadie learns of it...

No. My body spasms. *Just no*.

He doesn't get to take from her any more.

Not a fucking drop.

Not on my watch.

And the sooner I can get her and Lottie out of here, the better.

My phone buzzes in my pocket and I pull it out, jaw already locked.

Taylor.

I glance at Lottie, still engrossed in the TV, and back up into the kitchen before answering. 'Hey.'

'Hey...'

I flinch at the sound of her voice. So brittle. So unlike her.

'Can you talk?'

'Yeah. She's packing. How are you holding up?'

'I'll be a lot better once you've got her out of the city.'

Still that tremor in her voice. The terror. Just the thought of him breaking Tay the way he broke Sadie – two of the most important women in my life – I can't bear it.

'We'll be gone in a couple of hours.'

'Good. That's good.' A pause. 'Though even then... what's to say he won't—'

My fist clenches around the phone. Nails bite into my other palm.

'He won't find us. He has no way of tracking us there.'

Her breath shudders down the line. 'He said he could *smell* her on me, Theo.'

Ice slices through my spine.

'Actually *smell* her. Said it was her perfume, her shampoo... The freak said he'd know it anywhere.'

I swallow down bile, even as my inner voice accuses me of the same twisted skill. I'd know her anywhere. Difference being, I'd never hurt her. Not ever.

I'd kill for her, though. And that man...

'His days are numbered,' I bite out, teeth grinding so hard, it hurts. 'Axel's onto him, the police too. They'll get him.'

They have to. Because I can't think about the alternative.

'Until they do, she can't know about this,' Taylor whispers. 'You understand? If she knew he got to me, how close he'd come—'

'I know,' I cut in. 'I know.'

Because I do know.

It would destroy everything she's fought so hard to rebuild.

And I'd rather choke on the truth than see her broken again.

'Thank you, Theo. I don't know what we'd do without you.'

'Not a problem you need to worry about. You've got me. You both have, for as long as you need.'

And forever more too. Because one thing's brutally clear – now that Sadie's back in life, my heart won't let her go without a fight.

What that means... I'm too fucking terrified to admit.

But this isn't about how I feel. I tell myself the same as I told her. It's about how she feels.

Her life. Her freedom. Her and Lottie's path.

And whatever comes next, I'll walk it with them – even if it tears me in two at the end.

15

SADIE

And I thought Theo's penthouse was impressive.

Turns out his 'beach house' is something else entirely.

Perched high above a secluded cove, it's a blend of weathered wood, white-rendered walls, and sea-tinted glass. Stark and sculptural, yet somehow gentle, like it's always been here, surrounded by the driftwood and windswept dunes.

Inside, every room invites the landscape in, each one perfectly positioned to capture the golden cove below, or the restless, endless sea beyond.

From the moment Lottie and I stepped out of the car, we were wrapped in its beauty – and the warm, effusive welcome of Theo's live-in housekeeper, Isla. A grey-haired widow with the kindest smile and brightest blue eyes, who served us a feast for dinner, then took Lottie to see the chickens in the coop. Since then, it's been chicken this and chicken that and *all* the smiles.

Now, with Lottie finally settled in bed, I pad down the hallway in search of Theo, taking in every abstract coastal print on the white walls, every sculpted piece of driftwood nestled in the recessed shelves. Even the pale timber floor catches the eye, while the thrum of the sea fills the air like nature's own lullaby.

Pure heaven.

Though not as heavenly as the sight that greets me when I reach the living room.

The last of the evening sun filters through the glass walls and linen drapes, softening the room's clean lines and coastal tones... and him.

He's stretched out on the low-slung sofa, glass of wine in hand, phone resting forgotten beside him. The light turns his skin to honey, drawing out the textured tones in his dark-blond hair and the stubble along his jaw.

His white T-shirt and pale-blue jeans wear the day's creases, but somehow only add to the effect that's all him. He looks undone in the most effortless way. Like he belongs here. Like this place was designed with him in mind, which it was, and yet he rarely comes here. Or so Isla said in passing.

I hesitate in the doorway, unwilling to break his peace. But I fear Lottie will come for him, if he doesn't get to her first...

'I hate to ruin the mood,' I say gently, 'but she's asking for you...'

His eyes shift into focus, sharpening on me before softening with a smile. 'She is?'

I nod. 'She's almost gone, but I reckon she'll fight it until she gets a good-night from her Uncle Feo.'

He places his glass on the table and rises. 'Consider it done.'

As he passes, his hand brushes my hip – light, almost absent-minded, but enough to still my breath. For one suspended beat, I think he might lean in. Say something. Do something. But he just smiles and says, 'Help yourself to some wine. I won't be long.'

I watch him go, my cheeks too warm, my tummy too. I blame the car journey, being in such close proximity but with Lottie as a constant chaperone. Then Isla. But soon... we'll be alone.

Alone for the first time since last night... the flutters within me multiply and I move before he finds me stuck in the same spot, stuck in a stupor of my own making.

I pour myself a glass and step out onto the deck. Breathe in the view as dusk settles over the cove. I can't remember the last time I witnessed anything so quietly perfect and unspoiled by human touch.

I wrap my cardigan around me, letting the breeze thread through my hair, and sip my wine. It's a crisp, dry white. Refreshing, but it could never quench my thirst. Not when it's stirred by the man now returning, his footsteps soft on the wood behind me.

'She seems quite content here,' he says, wine in one hand, the other settling on the rail beside me. The sight of those fingers up close draws last night's touch back under my skin and I swallow, look back to the sea.

'Much like her mother,' I say thickly. 'It's so beautiful here... I can't believe you rarely visit.'

He looks out towards the sea with me, a small smile playing about his lips.

'Now you sound like *my* mother.'

'It was Isla who dropped you in it. She thinks it's a travesty that the place sits empty much of the time.'

'It doesn't sit empty. She lives here.'

'I think her point was more that you don't take time out to enjoy it. Like your mother, she probably worries that you work too hard and play too little.'

It's what I think too, but he promised not to judge me when it came to my life, and I owe him the same. Doesn't mean I can't pass on the message, though... and tease him a little along the way.

'Though if you ask me, it does feel mighty cruel on the rest of us, owning a place like this and not using it. If it were mine, I'd be here all the time.'

He grins down at me. 'Is that so?'

Turns out, the only person I'm teasing is myself. The picture paints itself so vividly – me, him, Lottie, here. Not just now, but...

I take a swig of wine, force it through my tightened throat. 'Who wouldn't.'

'I can think of a few.'

'Axel?'

He nods. 'Too quiet.'

'Taylor?'

He smiles. 'She'd manage a short stint, I reckon.'

'Katie?'

He coughs mid-sip of his wine. 'How did you— *Taylor*?'

'She may have let slip you had a fiancée...' I say it with all good humour, because it is. I shouldn't care that he has a past. Especially when I have my own... as questionable as mine is. And he's a thirty-seven-year-old guy who looks like he does, lives the life he does; I'd be more concerned if he didn't have one.

No, what does concern me is that no one has stuck. That according to Taylor, he's unable to share his life with another. And Lottie and I are living proof that's not true. And the fact that he owns a place as incredible as this and doesn't use it...

'I never brought Katie here.'

'But you did own it when she was around?' And to be engaged, she must have been around long enough; did he really come here that *little*?

He nods. 'I bought it just before dad died.' His gaze drifts to the view as he raises his wine glass to the cove. 'There's a small holiday cottage in the grounds, tucked away just down there. It's where my parents brought me every summer as a kid. When it came on the market, I figured, why not? The cottage was supposed to be a retirement gift to them both...'

'Oh, Theo.' My heart breaks. 'You never said anything about this place back then.'

He told me of his guilt. Of how much he missed his father and wished he'd been around more, wished for another family dinner, a conversation, just time. But this... to miss gifting him this.

'It wasn't much to write home about in those days. The cottage was in dire need of renovation and this place was a derelict outbuilding. I forgot about it all for a long time after Dad... Then a few years ago, the farm next door got in touch asking to buy the land and it gave me the kick I needed to sort it out. I paid a team to come in and refurb the cottage for Mum, redesign this place for me. I figured one day, I'd have the time to come and enjoy it.'

'I bet your mum loves it,' I say softly.

His eyes flicker over the horizon as he gives the faintest of smiles. 'Yeah, she does...' Then he clears his throat as his mouth quirks up. 'Katie, though, she was more your cocktails on the Côte d'Azur type than a glass of wine in Wales.'

'Your words or...?'

'I think hers were that it lacked in the essentials.'

I cock a brow. '*Essentials*?'

'Oh, you know – a pool, a fully-staffed spa...'

'Ri-ight.' I laugh into my glass. 'Taylor said you struggled to live with her. She didn't say she was high-maintenance, too.'

'And now you *definitely* sound like my mother. Are you sure you two haven't caught up behind my back?'

'Promise,' I say with a slow smile, daring to press, 'So is that why you two didn't work out? She was *too much* for you.'

He gives a tight laugh. 'There were many reasons we didn't work. If you ask Katie, she'd say I was already married to my job.'

Of all the reasons he could give, that one lands the hardest. Because for a man who'd been determined to see his parents work less and live more, Katie's reason reaffirms what everyone else has said: that he's fallen into the same trap.

Doesn't matter what I've witnessed in him these last few weeks, seeing him put me and Lottie first. We're a temporary distraction, a momentary blip in his routine, and I don't doubt for a second he'll return to it when we're gone. Return to it and then some, making up for the time he's lost.

I want so desperately to say something, but... no judgement.

'And what about you?' I say gently, trying a different tack. 'What would you say the reason was?'

His eyes don't leave the horizon, but something in his posture shifts. I start to think he's not going to answer at all, when finally, he speaks.

'Before Dad died, work was a way to secure the future for all of us. After... it filled a void that nothing else could fill. Not even Katie.' He turns to me, the weight behind his eyes making it hard to breathe. 'So, no. It wasn't that she was too much. It's that I wasn't enough to give her what she needed.'

The confession hangs in the air, raw and real.

But all I can think is that the man I've come to know again has been more than enough for me. More than enough for me *and* for Lottie.

'Or maybe she wasn't what you needed to be able to give that to?'

His eyes narrow and I feel my heart slow, the meaning of what I've just said registering and settling in my chest. How foolish, revealing, and stupid stupid stupid.

'But hey, what do I know? I'm hardly the relationship expert, am I?' I chuckle into my wine, taking a sip and trying not to choke on my foolishness. 'I have to say though, if I had to choose between the Côte d'Azur and this...'

I set my glass on the rail, fingers curling around the wood as I fix my gaze on everything Wales currently has on offer. The sun is just a deep-pink sliver now, its shifting hues rippling across the water as waves whisper against the burnished shore.

I breathe it in deep. Let it out slow. Feel the calm overtake me...

'I'd choose this every time.' I smile. Accepting it for what it is. My current reality. My life in this moment. 'Because this, Theo. This is perfection.'

And I'm happy. For the first time in too long, I'm actually happy.

Not just free and living, but happy.

And all the crazy flutterings he stirs up inside me, they're just noise above that totally exquisite baseline of H-A-P-P-Y.

'Yeah,' he murmurs beside me, his voice lower, heavier – like he's just waking up to the beauty he's overlooked all this time. 'It really is.'

Only... he's not looking at the view at all. He's looking straight at me. And the way he says it... the way his eyes look... they have that burn, the same fire he was sporting on his knees last night...

My breath catches and I think about the promise I made to myself that morning.

To take what hadn't been perfect and make it so.

By claiming his mouth and his pleasure, too.

'Theo?'

* * *

Theo

She's got that look in her eye.

The one that says she's thinking things I shouldn't be entertaining.

Not when she just called me out over Katie. Hit me with a question so sharp, it carved right through the lie I've been living with, like she didn't even know it was my deepest fear laid bare.

And Axel's voice echoes behind hers:

'Maybe it's just easier to hide behind work than admit you've been stuck on the same girl for almost ten years.'

She can't know.

Because I don't know.

Not for sure.

And if I screw this up – if I chase a feeling I've never dared name – I don't just risk breaking myself. I risk ruining her. And I brought her here to prevent Danny from doing just that. To protect everything she's rebuilt – so fragile and hard-earned, it's fucking sacred.

She looks happy. Whole, even. And the idea that *I* could undo that, send her spiralling back to the girl by the river... worse, the cowering woman from the park.

No. Fuck, no.

'We should go inside,' I mutter, voice rough, already half-turned to leave.

But she stops me, her palm pressing against my chest, and every nerve lights up.

My eyes find hers. And then I'm looking at her – *really* looking. Caught in the fire of her gaze, the colour in her cheeks, the sheen of her lips...

'This morning, I made a promise to myself.'

'Yeah?' I rasp, my voice already betraying me.

She nods slowly, the breeze picking up around us – lifting strands of her hair, sending her cardigan slipping off one shoulder. My gaze follows it, drawn helplessly to the exposed skin, the soft curve of her breast just visible. My fingers twitch, my mouth dries up – wanting to touch, to taste, to trace...

She doesn't move. Doesn't cover up. Like she knows what it's costing me, and she's daring me to look away, to walk away from this.

And God help me, I can't.

'I promised myself that the next time I took my pleasure, you were coming with me.'

Fuck. My jaw locks, my cock bucking against my jeans all too willing to agree.

'I'm supposed to be protecting you,' I grind out.

'From what, the seagulls?' She gives a breathy laugh, the heat of her continued touch seeping through the fabric of my tee. 'Because last I checked, we're completely alone.'

'You know what I mean.'

'I don't,' she says, her voice soft but unwavering. 'Because I feel safe, Theo. Safer than I've felt in years.'

But she wasn't safe. Not even twenty-four hours ago. And that truth – hidden from her but pounding inside me – is a blade against my ribs.

'And it's because of you,' she adds, her palm sliding up to my neck, fingers toying with the hair there, and it takes everything I have not to groan. 'You didn't just give us shelter, you gave me the confidence to get out there and live my life again. You helped me remember who I am. You helped me see the kind of woman I want to be. Strong. Sure. A good mother that Lottie can look up to.'

'You were *always* a good mum, don't ever doubt that,' I burst out, my fingers threading through her hair as I urge her to see it. 'And you did all that by yourself.'

'I couldn't have done it without you.' Her voice breaks, just slightly. 'You believed in me. You pushed me.'

'You wouldn't have needed pushing if that bastard—'

She covers my mouth with her thumb, eyes bright with unshed tears. 'Not tonight. I don't want to talk about him tonight. I just want to thank you. And maybe... maybe claim a few more stars.'

Stars. *Fuck.* That claiming lives in my soul.

And it's in hers too. Her eyes blaze with it, while her words – the gentle hope...

Her hand trembles as I take it from my mouth and press it between us, just to feel her there. To stop myself from ruining this with all the things I still don't know how to say.

'I don't want to hurt you, Sadie. If I screw this up— if I get this wrong—'

'You won't. You can't break me. Trust me. I've been broken. And now I'm stronger than ever.' She inhales softly, her eyes holding me captive with her words. 'I'm strong enough to enjoy this for what it is. And walk away when it's over. No promises. No expectations. My life with Lottie comes first. Always.'

I see it: the truth in her. No hesitation. No fear. Only fire.

And still, I hesitate.

She tilts her head, leans in the barest inch. 'Give me the stars again, Theo, and I'll promise you some of your own...'

My pulse hammers in my throat. Every inch of my body screams to close the space between us. To forget everything outside this moment – every reason I told myself I couldn't, shouldn't, wouldn't.

But she's here.

And she's not begging, she's claiming this moment. Hers. Mine. Making it ours.

She reaches up and gently takes the wine glass from my hand, sets it down beside hers on the rail. Then – barely brushing – her lips sweep across mine. Intentionally soft, breathtakingly electrifying.

'But this time...' she whispers, 'I want your kiss, too.'

Her tongue flicks lightly against my bottom lip—

Fuck.

I snap, smothering the curse as I crush my mouth to hers. My tongue sweeps inside, an invasion that claims me more than it ever could her. She tastes of wine and everything I was never meant to touch. So right. So wrong.

But I've wanted this for so damn long, and now that I have it, my body isn't mine any more. It's carnal instinct, fierce and out of control.

I drag her to me with both hands – one tangled in her hair, the other fisted in her cardigan. She gasps as I press her up against the rail. Desperate to feel her everywhere, all at once. Restraint obliterated, I kiss her again. And again. Deeper. Rougher. My hands roam – her hair, her waist, her spine – gripping, pulling, needing.

And she meets me head-on. All heat and surrender and everything I never let myself hope for…

There's no holding back.

No *going* back.

This isn't safe.

This isn't smart.

This is *inevitable*.

And I want all of it.

Even if it wrecks me in the process.

'Bedroom,' I command. 'Now.'

* * *

Sadie

I shake my head, not wanting to break the spell. Not even for a second.

I know Lottie's asleep. I know Isla's in her quarters. It's just us.

And there's no way in hell I'm giving him time to reconsider.

'Here,' I say in the same tone. 'Now.'

His breath shudders against my lips, but he doesn't move.

So I do.

I slide my hands beneath his shirt, desperate to feel every inch of him – the body I've dreamed of, fantasised about, the man I've wanted for so long.

I rake my fingers over his abs, up his chest, dragging his shirt with me. He trembles as I strip it from him, letting it drop to the ground, my cardigan with it.

His eyes fall to my body, dark and molten as he lowers his head. He kisses my neck, my collarbone, my shoulder – stubble grazing, teeth scraping. I shiver, hot and cold in the same instant. He hooks his fingers into the straps of my dress, easing them down my arms until gravity takes over and it pools at my feet.

The sea breeze filters through the lace of my bra, a teasing whisper over heated skin. He unfastens the clasp, and I tilt my head back. Dizzy with anticipation. Undone by sensation.

My bra slips away, and he lets out a low, reverent curse as my breasts spill free. My nipples tighten, straining towards the cool night air and the heat of his stare.

'So fucking beautiful,' he murmurs, and my whole body blooms under his appreciation, craving his touch as his hands glide over me.

He palms the swell of my breasts, thumbs teasing their hardened peaks until I can't catch a full breath. My body arcs back, my hips shifting with a need so raw, I cry his name.

'Please, Theo.' I pull his mouth back to mine, tasting the groan that rumbles deep within his chest, feeling the strain in his shoulders, the restraint he's barely holding onto. But I don't want restraint. Not now.

As the salt-tinged air whips around us, I lean into his heat and tell him what he needs to know: 'I'm on the pill.'

His eyes flare – hot, wide, *wrecked*.

'And I want you here,' I whisper.

His breath hitches, and for a beat, we stare at each other, like the weight of what's about to happen is too big to name.

Then he moves. Sweeping me up and setting me down on the table. His hands go to the fly of his jeans, popping the button, and I trap my bottom lip between my teeth as I stare – hungry, enraptured.

'You need to stop looking at me like that,' he growls, hands stilling.

'Like what?'

'Like you want to eat me.'

I press my lips together and meet his gaze.

'But I do.'

His curse is a hiss I feel deep in my core. I take over for him, tugging his zipper down, dragging denim and boxers over his hips...

The second he springs free – hard, flushed, perfect – I'm licking my lips, eyes begging. 'Please.'

His jaw clenches in answer, every muscle carved like stone as I wrap my fingers around him. One stroke, and he bucks, pre-cum already beading at the tip. I slip to my knees and scoop it up with my tongue. He groans out my name, his hands fisting in my hair. Rough. Weak. Losing it for me.

I sink my mouth over him, tongue curling around his breadth, my hand moving in rhythm. Every inch of him – mine.

I suck back, and his thighs tremble.

'*Sadie...*'

I look up, my murmured, 'Yes,' vibrating around his length as his body pulses, his release close. So close.

'Get up here,' he grinds out.

I draw back slowly, giving him one last stroke – tight, purposeful – relishing the sound that rips from his throat, the taste of his impending climax on my tongue, the way he's coming apart just for me.

Then he's grabbing my waist, thrusting me onto the table.

'You'll be the death of me,' he hisses, and my inner devil preens as he tears my knickers away.

His gaze rakes over me and I lean back, soaking it in. There's reverence there, but it's laced with something darker. Possessive. Intense.

His hands trail up my thighs, fingers skimming between my legs slowly, torturously, and I part for him. Letting him see how wet I am. How desperate.

He thumbs my clit, his eyes burning into his touch, and my hips roll with my groan. *More, please more.* And he answers my silent plea, his fingers dipping inside as his thumb continues to roll.

'So fucking beautiful,' he repeats. His other hand smooths up my side to cup my breast, teasing the pleading peak before his mouth comes down to greet it. He draws it in – tongue flicking, mouth sucking. His teeth nip, gently... then harder. *Oh, yes.* I clutch his shoulders, my body shamelessly arching, urging him for more.

He palms my breast while still feasting on the other, his tantalising caress between my legs pushing me to the brink. Every limb tightens. I'm going, and I want him with me.

I sink my hands into his hair, yanking every strand as I tug him to my mouth.

'I want you, Theo. I want you now.'

He plunders my lips, all heat and hunger as he spreads my thighs with his body and tugs me to him. His tip nudges at my entrance and his head rocks back, eyes locking with mine... this is it. God, yes. This is it. No going back.

'*Take me.*'

He thrusts forward – one powerful stroke – and he's buried deep. I see it in his eyes, feel it in my heart. He's taking my all, in the most beautiful, soul-crushing way. And I refuse to fear it.

I wrap my legs around him, arms too, pulling him impossibly closer as I find his mouth, claiming his kiss as he claims my body and more.

I gasp his name, open my eyes, and find his still blazing down on me. It's everything. *He's* everything. This man I once thought I'd lost forever – now, he's here, inside me, around me, mine.

For tonight, at least, he's mine.

And I let go of everything but this.

This moment.

This man.

And as we claim the stars together, I know they'll stay with me forever...

Even if *he* won't.

16

THEO

I wake to the soft tap of keys.

Not a sound I've ever woken up to before.

It takes a second to place it.

Then I remember.

I'm not alone. *Sadie.*

My eyes snap open.

The pale light of dawn spills across the room. The linen curtains billow gently in the breeze drifting through the open sliding doors – and there she is.

Out on the balcony, laptop open, lip caught between her teeth, lost in whatever she's working on. She's wrapped in my robe, legs curled beneath her, hair wild from sleep... and me.

Desire floods my body as my mind brands the sight to memory, knowing it's something I'll ache for long after it's gone.

She must sense my gaze because she looks over. Her smile is slow, small, and totally my undoing. I lift the edge of the quilt in silent invitation and her smile deepens. She closes her laptop and pads over to me. Places the device on the bedside table and without a word, shrugs the robe from her shoulders.

Now *that* is the greatest wake-up call known to man.

Forget coffee. Sadie. Naked. Lit up by the morning sun. Mine. All mine.

I grab her hand and pull her into bed with a low growl. 'Too slow.'

She laughs softly, straddling me with purpose, her mouth already finding mine. 'You're insatiable.'

'I'll show you insatiable.' I roll her under me and leave her in no doubt of how much I want her, how much I'm going to keep wanting her until she tells me to stop.

And when she does, I'll step back. I'll watch her walk away.

And I'll do it without a fight.

Because *this*... this will always be hers to end.

Even if it breaks something in me I'll never get back.

* * *

Sadie

'What are we going to tell Lottie?'

We're sipping coffee at the breakfast bar. The fresh morning air drifts in through the open French doors, carrying Lottie's distant chatter with it when Theo asks the question. Isla's taken Lottie to collect eggs and feed the animals – goats as well as chickens, much to Lottie's delight – so his timing doesn't surprise me. His expression does.

I set my phone down, which has been blowing up with blog updates, and bite my lip to hold back a laugh.

'It's not funny.'

'It is when you're blushing because of it.'

'I'm not blushing.'

I give him a pointed stare and he rakes a hand through his hair, his bicep flexing against another white tee – yeah, I might have admitted last night how thirsty his white T-shirts make me. Or more specifically, him in them.

'Okay, fine. I'm blushing.'

He really is. And it's totes adorable.

'Just answer the question.'

'She's three, Theo. She'll think you're keeping mummy's bed warm and making her happy. All true.'

'So it won't confuse her?'

His tone shifts – gently, but enough.

Coffee forgotten, I fold my hands in my lap and hold his gaze. 'She won't suddenly start thinking you're her new daddy, if that's what you mean. Or at least, I don't think she will. She barely knew Danny existed, and she never asks about him.'

His eyes darken at the mention of Danny, his hand curling into a fist upon the table. But the sight doesn't strike fear in me – not like it would have with Danny. I trust Theo. I know he'd never hurt me. Not like that. And it's not the sight of his anger I mind. It's the weight of it. The hurt he carries – for Lottie, for me, maybe for the part of himself that wasn't there when I needed someone. Not that he could have known.

'That's the one silver lining of him being so ignorant of her,' I murmur. 'She doesn't feel the hole, because he never gave her anything to miss...'

And then it hits me, full force.

'Much like how my own father...' I swallow the sudden pang in my chest. 'Funny how life has a tendency to repeat itself.'

Theo's eyes soften into mine. 'You're everything she needs, Sadie.'

I hold his gaze, the past coming back to me like it happened only yesterday. The riverbank, his words...

'That's not what you thought about *me* seven years ago...'

His head lifts slightly.

'You said I saw you as some kind of substitute.'

His eyes flicker as he registers my meaning. 'I'm sorry for what I said back then. If I could take it back, I would. But you were so young—'

'I was an adult.'

'Twelve years younger—'

'Newsflash,' I say with a wry smile, 'I'm still twelve years younger.'

He huffs a breath, jaw working. 'But it's different now.'

I cock a brow. 'Is it?'

His eyes trail over me, stripped of anything but the truth. 'No.' It comes out gruff, pained, honest. 'I wanted you then. And I want you still.'

Holy fuck. Of all the things he could have said. Of all the things I *expected* him to say. It wasn't that. My own words, my own meaning repeated back at me. And my heart's not prepared for it. My walls are not high enough.

'I hated myself back then,' he says, 'for wanting you like I did. But I can't hate myself for it now. Whatever this is... I'm all in. For as long as you need me to be.'

What if I asked him for forever, would he give it to me?

Because that look in his eye says yes. The way he anchored me to him last night, this morning... it *all* felt like yes.

But I *can't* ask for forever.

Because I'm the one who promised it was for *now*.

The one who said my life with Lottie came first, always.

And I'm only just getting my life back; pushing too hard, too soon, for something this new, this untested, this delicate... knowing what I know of him, his inability to give that part of himself away. I'm cross I'm even contemplating it, when I should be cherishing what he *is* giving me.

So I push all thought of the future aside, and slip behind the now...

'Until then, *Uncle Feo*,' I say, quietly teasing, 'we'll just tell Lottie that you're my *special* friend.'

His brows lift, his mouth following. 'Special, huh?'

'*Very special.*'

He grins, grabbing me by the waist and pulling me into his lap. His lips find mine in a kiss that's far too devilish for the breakfast table.

'Ew!'

We spring apart.

Two faces stare at us through the open French doors. Lottie smothers her mouth, half-giggling, half-grossed out, while Isla's eyes twinkle bright.

'Well, well, well...' she says, sounding more Welsh than ever, one hand in Lottie's, the other cradling a basket brimming with eggs as they walk on in. 'Not sure whether I should tell the pair of you to wash your mouth out with soap or hose you down with cold water.'

'*Soap?*' Lottie scrunches up her face, looking properly disgusted now, and we all laugh.

'Either way,' Isla says, 'it looks to me like you've already had your fill for breakfast.'

'I don't know about that, Mrs P,' Theo says, his arm still deliciously hot and possessive around my waist. 'I think I'm going to need the fuel.'

My eyes flare wide, my heart somersaulting as I kick him in the shin.

Now *I'm* the one turning crimson.

Isla chuckles all the more. 'Hear that, Lottie? Our efforts won't go to waste. Now hop up here and get those hands washed, you're on chef duty with me.'

I watch them, Isla's arm slipping easily around Lottie's tiny shoulders, guiding her towards the sink like they've done this a dozen times before. And just like that, my daughter's giggling, caught in the glow of someone who sees her, includes her, practically loves her already.

A lump catches in my throat before I can swallow it. Danny's parents were long gone before I met him. I know nothing about them... except what they raised. Not that I blame them. I blame *him*.

But still, Lottie's never known a grandparent. Never had anyone of that generation spoil her in that way, just because...

Theo's voice comes soft beside me. 'Hey, you okay?'

I nod quickly, dashing an escaped tear from my cheek with the back of my hand and smiling wide. 'Yeah... Isla's amazing with her.'

'She should be,' he murmurs, his hand caressing my side, gifting me the comfort I haven't asked for, but he knows I need. 'She's got ten grandkids of her own. Most of them local. She splits her time between here and helping out with them.' He pauses, adding for my ears only, 'Her husband passed away not long before she came to work for me. She wanted something to help keep her busy. A new environment to be in.'

The ache in his words reflects something deeper. I know what he's thinking: his dad, the void, filling it with work. Our grief may be shaped differently, but it echoes just the same.

I intertwine my fingers with his against my side, press my other hand over the top.

'So Lottie,' he calls out, 'you fancy going to the beach after breakfast?'

I think even the cows in the next field heard her answer...

* * *

Theo

'Not so far ahead, darling!' Sadie hollers, a half-laugh in her voice as Lottie tears across the beach, her tiny feet kicking up wet sand. The kite I bought her – a blaze of colour – whips through the sky like it's got somewhere better to be.

Though I'm pretty sure nowhere on earth could beat this right now.

'It's f'ying, Mummy!' she shrieks with joy, her little legs pumping like she could catch the clouds. 'It's f'ying!'

'She'll be all right,' I murmur, the sight tugging at my chest. 'Gotta let her be a kid. It's why we're here, to let her run wild, right?'

And the rest, my head unhelpfully supplies. But I won't let the guilt set in. Not when they're so happy, and it *feels* this right.

'Yeah.'

Sadie's smile lingers on Lottie, her blue eyes bright and alive, her hair a chaotic tumble of waves... She looks every inch the mum on holiday. Or a woman who spent the night... *and don't go there. Not if you want to avoid sporting a semi in public!*

A cheer goes up from a group of lads mid-footie match, and I reach instinctively for her hand. But her smile doesn't waver.

A dog skirts by, close, barking. Not even a flinch.

'It's hard to believe she's the same girl,' Sadie says softly, her eyes still on Lottie.

'She's not,' I say. 'And neither are you. You're both... brighter, stronger.'

I thread my fingers through hers and she smiles up at me.

'Happy?'

Yeah, it catches in my throat as I nod. So much going on within me and I can't put words to any of it. *Can't or won't?*

'Though I reckon she's going to face plant any second,' she says, shaking her head.

'She'll bounce,' I assure her. 'She's built like her mum. Tough.'

'Oh, cheers!' She laughs, rolling her eyes. But there's no edge to it. Just warmth.

The breeze shifts, bringing the scent of salt and seaweed and something else – something old. Childhood, maybe. Probably. It's the kind of peace I haven't felt in years. Maybe ever. And the past – memories from before Dad died, before work swallowed everything – it's still there. But it doesn't ache like it used to.

'I took my fair share of tumbles out here when I was her age,' I say. 'Didn't do me any harm.'

She looks at me with that soft, tilted smile. 'I'd have liked to see that.'

'You still can,' I say, tugging her hand. 'Come on.'

She stumbles into the run with me, laughing again as we chase Lottie down the shoreline, water kicking up around our feet.

Three pairs of prints in the wet sand.

Three voices tangled in the wind.

The happiest of trios... almost like a—

No, don't go there.

But it's hard not to.

Maybe it's the childhood memories creeping in, or the families scattered up and down the beach.

Or maybe it's the night we spent together.

Either way, the thought is there.

And I'm not entirely sure I want to quash it.

* * *

Sadie

Lottie falls asleep brushing her teeth.

It's one of the sweetest, funniest, most endearing sights I've ever seen. Though I have to say, when I find Theo asleep on the sofa after tucking her in, I'm a little torn between the two.

Both wiped out after a day at the seaside.

Both wearing the same wind-kissed glow.

Same small smiles.

My heart beats warm and fast beneath my ribs, and I press a palm to my chest, hold onto the moment for a second longer, before my buzzing phone cuts in.

I know what it is before I even check. The site. It's taking off fast. And I'm barely keeping up with the day-to-day. The emails, the chatter, the feature requests, the potential sponsors piling in...

But like any mum knows, while the house sleeps, you can get shit done.

And I lose track of time as I take my laptop out to the deck and work. Not that the site has ever felt like work-work. More a passion that requires time and thought. And when the moonlit sea is your backdrop, it's pretty damn close to paradise.

'Hey...'

Correction. *Now* it's paradise.

Theo stands in the open doorway, face soft from sleep, hair all tousled. My breath catches as my core clenches – how is it possible to want him again already? And *this* deeply?

'Hey, you okay?' I ask, sliding my laptop onto the table and patting the bench, telling him to join me.

He nods and eases down next to me, one arm draping along my back, warming me from top to toe. 'How long was I out?'

'No idea. But you clearly needed it.'

He ruffles his hair with a sheepish grin. 'It's all that fresh air.'

'And you didn't get much sleep last night...'

Not that my body's complaining, it's already burning for round two.

'I don't see you suffering.'

'I'm a mum. I function on zero sleep and way too much caffeine.'

He chuckles. 'Yeah, I bet.' He smooths the hair from my shoulder, eyes following the move. 'You should've woken me up.'

'And spoil...' a gasp slips out as his lips brush my neck '...your beauty sleep?'

'You saying I *need* beauty sleep now?' he murmurs against my skin, then nips.

I shiver and whimper.

'Never,' I breathe.

'Good girl...' His hand falls to my thigh, slipping beneath the hem of my skirt.

'Theo!'

He hums in response.

'We shouldn't, not here...'

'Last I checked, we were alone, remember? And I'm not suggesting we get naked this time.' His fingers travel higher, grazing the lace of my thong, and my legs part, wanting, needing... 'I'm merely gifting you more stars.'

My head falls back as I clutch the edge of the bench and his mouth finds the hollow behind my ear – breath teasing, tongue slow and wicked. His fingers move over the lace. Circling. Lazy at first. Every stroke deliberate. A tease, meant to build. To pull.

He's not rushing. He doesn't need to. He knows exactly what he's doing and my hips lift of their own accord – chasing more, needing more – the pleasure climbing with every breathless second. Until it's all I can feel. All I can breathe.

And then I'm gone. My climax crashing through me in wave after blinding wave as I cry out his name to the stars and thank each and every one of them for this.

For him.

* * *

Theo

I can never get enough of making Sadie come.

Having her cry out my name is like being trusted with something rare, something holy – the way she lets go with me, the way she lets herself feel.

Especially when I compare it to the haunted look on her face just minutes ago...

'That's better,' I say, wrapping my arm around her and drawing her into my side.

'*Better?*'

'You looked so serious when I came out, I was worried you were...' I don't need to say it for her to understand – I thought she was thinking about him.

'No, not at all. I was working.'

She's been working a lot, I've noticed. On her phone, on her laptop – every spare moment, she's checking something. I figured it was a habit. Always needing to be plugged it. And yeah, I get that. This is me, after all. But we're supposed to be taking a break.

'What about being on holiday?'

'This kind of work doesn't really sleep.'

I frown, something in the way she says it making me sit up and take notice. 'What kind of work?'

She bites her lip and my neck prickles.

'Sadie?'

She glances at her laptop, now asleep, and swipes a finger across the trackpad. 'This.'

I glance at the screen as it lights up, and my eyes widen. She's on a forum about domestic abuse. Stories. Resources. Comments. Support threads. Danny's still haunting her – even now, even here. My gut rolls.

'You're reaching out for help...'

'No.' Her voice is steady. 'I'm giving it. This is my site, Theo. All of it. No one knows it's me. It's been my secret... until now.'

Something within me unravels, a light turning on somewhere deep. 'You went from vlogging about cosmetics to blogging about abuse?'

'In a nutshell, yeah.'

'Why didn't you say anything?'

She gives a soft, shaky breath. 'I don't know. I was so used to keeping it secret in the early days for obvious reasons. And then, even after I got away, I still couldn't shake the shame. Or the blame. I carried it around like a shadow. Hiding behind a screen let me be honest in a way I couldn't be out loud.'

It guts me to hear her talk like that: the shame, the blame. Even with those feelings behind her, I can't stop thinking about the scars they've left behind. And I hate that I can't take them from her. Can't erase them. Can't make her whole without them.

But then... she wouldn't have created this.

I scroll through the site – post after post, pages of thoughtful resources, personal essays, guides, interviews. The comment sections full of gratitude, of people saying, *This helped me, I thought I was alone, you gave me hope.*

'Sadie... this is huge.'

She nods slowly. 'Bigger than I ever imagined.'

I turn to look at her, and it's like seeing her all over again. The strength. The heart. The quiet determination to take something that broke her and use it to build something that might save someone else.

'You are incredible.'

She gives a breathy laugh. 'I wouldn't go that far.'

'To come out of all you've been through and give back like this?' I shake my head, full of something way deeper than pure admiration. 'You don't even see it, do you? You didn't just survive – you're changing lives.'

'I hope so.'

'I know so. You should be so proud of all you've achieved.'

'Now you really are going too far.'

'No.' I lift her chin, holding her gaze to mine. 'I once told you I'd believe in you coming back – stronger, smarter, more beautiful than ever – until you could. And you did it. Now I'll be proud of you, until you can be proud of yourself.'

And then I kiss her before I say the one thing there's no coming back from.

Because this is about her – always has been, always will be.

My feelings don't come into it.

17

SADIE

I'm alone in the house.

Isla's taken Lottie to visit her grandkids in the village, and Theo's gone for a run along the beach. I wanted to go with him, but I've neglected my site enough as it is – putting time with Lottie first, and, if I'm being totally honest, Theo too.

It's been almost two weeks since we came to Pembrokeshire, and I'm not afraid to admit that they've been the best two weeks of my entire life. Every day has been its own little adventure, for me just as much as Lottie.

And I'm pretty sure it's been the same for Theo.

There's more colour in his cheeks, he's quicker to smile, quicker to laugh... If I'm glowing, then he's... what's the male equivalent?

Sunshine wrapped in stubble.

My laugh echoes through the quiet, and I realise how strange it feels to be alone.

I haven't been since we got here.

By night, we share a bed, unable to get enough of each other.

By day, we play like your everyday tourists. Knights and princesses in the castle. Hide and seek in the forest. Football on the beach. Crabbing in the rock pools. Eating more ice cream than any adult should ever admit to. And laughing until our bellies ache – purely from the laughing, not the ice cream. *Yeah, right.*

We make the happiest of trios, and I know what people must think when they see us. Because I see it too, when my guard is down and I'm not thinking too hard.

A family. A real, honest-to-God family. Just one more happy group in a sea of summer families.

And every time I remember we're not, my chest aches. It's not intentional. It just is.

That's the other reason I didn't go running with Theo this morning. We need space. *I* need space. Because all those outings... all those nights tangled in his sheets... all those blurred lines... They're starting to feel real.

Dangerously real.

The temptation to want, to hope, to believe it could be something more... it's getting harder to ignore.

Because Theo is everything I'd ever want in a partner.

Everything I'd ever want in a father for Lottie.

He's funny. He's kind. He's patient and thoughtful.

Smokin' hot, and downright filthy when he wants to be.

The way he looks at me. The way he *touches* me. The way he knows exactly when to be gentle and when to be anything but.

Is it any wonder I'm weak at the knees, day after day?

A part of me never wants this trip to end. But another part – the quieter, braver part – knows it has to. And soon. We said the summer and the summer's ending.

I need to keep moving forward. Free of Danny. Free of Theo, too.

Because the longer I stay wrapped up in his warmth, the more I fear I won't *want* to stand on my own. And I *have* to. I have to know that I can stand tall – even without him. *Especially* without him.

I step onto the deck and catch sight of him coming up the coastal path, wind in his hair, running clothes clinging in ways that should be illegal, and just like that, my heart goes on its merry dance, and my lips curve up.

I can't temper my reaction to him, so I don't even try. It's the flicker of hope I seek to kill off: the one that ponders the way he looks at me, the way he holds Lottie like she's his own. The hope that starts to wonder if he feels it too. The pull. The shift. The terrifying, dazzling promise of something more.

That maybe this life we've built in the span of two short weeks isn't just a holiday dream. Maybe it's a glimpse of what could be.

And oh my God, how wonderful that would be. How wonderful and perfect and maybe, just maybe... it really *could* be.

I raise a hand in a wave, but he doesn't see me. He's on the phone, talking into his earpiece. Working, probably.

Which is what you *should be doing.*

I sigh, head back inside, and open my laptop.

Emails first. And then... maybe a welcome-home kiss for Theo.

My inbox pings open – spam, newsletters, the usual avalanche. I start skimming through, finger hovering over delete when one subject line jumps out:

Subject: Your Story Is Changing Lives – We'd Be Honoured to Help You Share It Further!

I pause. The sender looks legit and the email itself... My stomach does a slow, stunned flip.

Dear Anon,

I'm Lucile Baldwin, an acquisitions editor at Empowered Publishing.

We've had the privilege of reading your blog and seeing firsthand the extraordinary reach and impact of your voice. Despite the understandable steps you've taken to protect your identity, it's clear to anyone reading that you once lived a public life as a successful vlogger. Something you were forced to give up, and yet here you are, reclaiming your story, post by powerful post.

You've created more than a blog; you've sparked a movement. Your words are helping others recognise abuse, name their experiences, and seek help. The comments speak volumes: people are opening up, connecting, finding the help they need because of you.

We believe we can help you extend your reach even further and would love to offer you a publishing deal, entirely on your terms. Whether you remain anonymous, use a pseudonym, or step back into the public eye, we'll support your comfort and safety every step of the way. If you choose to go public, we'll provide full media, marketing, and PR support to ensure it's done on your terms. Protected and supported every step of the way.

We're prepared to offer a competitive financial package, including an advance, royalties, and full editorial support to help shape your story, whether as a memoir, guide, or something entirely your own.

If you're open to a conversation, I'd love to speak further. We're also happy to host you at our London HQ, with full accommodation and care. There's no pressure, just an open door, when and if you're ready.

With deep respect,

Lucile Baldwin

Editorial Director

Empowered Publishing

Oh. My. God.

It's like everything I've been building towards without even realising it.

Like being handed a dream job you never knew you wanted.

And suddenly, I know, I want this.

More than that, I'm ready.

I'm done hiding. I want to stand tall and face the world. I want to own what happened to me. And give others like me a reason to hope. A reason to fight for something better.

Danny can't hurt me any more. I am strong. I am smart. I *am* enough.

And I can do this.

Share my voice. My truth. As *me*.

And for the first time in a long time, I feel it – faint but unmistakable.

Pride.

The very thing Theo promised to carry until I could carry it myself.

And the hope for a future together flares with my joy...

I'm already moving for the door, desperate to share this news with the one man who believed in me when I couldn't.

The one man who made all of this feel possible.

The one man I want in my future and always.

Theo.

* * *

Theo

'It's been two weeks, Axel. How the hell is he still out there?'

I pace the coastal path, every step grinding the frustration deeper. Two weeks. Two whole weeks since Danny vanished after blindsiding Taylor. And still, no arrest. No sighting. No news.

To anyone watching, I probably look like some deranged jogger, ranting at himself. But I don't care. I want answers. The right ones. The ones that see Danny behind bars and Sadie, free. Properly, free.

'He went dark after Taylor. He must have someone local he can hole up with, but all known contacts are cold. We'd have better intel if Sadie was—'

'No,' I snap. 'She'd know something's off. Taylor said to keep it quiet, and she's right.'

Is she? Are you sure *about that?*

'And if that blows up in your face?'

I rake a hand through my hair as the wind picks up, the sea crashing harder than it has in days. The sun's gone and there are dark clouds rolling in on the horizon... a storm I feel building within me too.

Maybe it's not just that he's still roaming free. Maybe it's that I let him become this... a twisted secret between us.

'Hell, I don't know any more, Axel. But I know I can't keep her holed up here forever...'

Though the thought of taking her back to London, knowing he's still out there...

Or is it the idea of taking her back and ending what you've found here that terrifies you more?

'Better there than here,' Axel says. 'Taylor's strung out enough without stressing about her sister being anywhere near him.'

'How is she? Taylor?'

Silence.

'Axel?'

'She's Taylor,' he clips out. 'She's as fierce as they come.'

'She didn't sound fierce, not when she called me the morning after he got—'

'*Theo?*'

The soft voice comes from behind me and my stomach drops. My eyes slam shut.

'Yeah,' Axel says in my ear, 'but she—'

'I've gotta go,' I cut him off, heart slamming as I turn. '*Sadie...*'

She's standing there, hair billowing in the breeze, white cotton shirt billowing with it – *my* white cotton shirt. Everything I want and everything I'm about to break.

'What's going on, Theo?'

She wraps her arms around her middle, and I can already see it in her eyes: the hurt I'm about to inflict with the secret I can no longer keep.

'Answer me.'

'Hear me out, okay.' I raise a desperate hand. 'Before you react, just let me explain.'

'I'm listening.'

'What did you hear?'

Her brows lift, eyes sharp and piercing, stabbing at my heart. 'I heard enough, now I want the whole story.'

'Sadie...'

'Don't "Sadie", me.' Her voice trembles. '*This* is about me. The least you can do is tell me everything.'

I swallow hard. 'Danny's in London... or he was.'

Her lashes flutter. 'When?'

'He— he was waiting outside Taylor's apartment the night you two met for drinks.'

She goes still. So very still, it's like the world stops with her. 'He got to Taylor?'

I nod and her throat bobs, fear widening her gaze.

'Is she—'

'She's okay,' I hurry out. 'He shook her up, but she's okay.'

Her face tightens. 'Why didn't you say anything? Why didn't *she* say anything?'

'I— We didn't want to upset you.'

Her jaw clenches, nostrils flaring. 'He *hurt* my sister, and *you* didn't want to upset me?' Then her mouth falls open on a gasp. 'Oh my God! That night – that was the day before you brought us here. You... Your sudden need to get us on holiday... You wanted to get us away from him?'

'Yes.' I rub the back of my neck, heart pounding as I fight to keep my voice steady. 'I couldn't risk him getting to you too. You were doing so well, and I wanted to protect that, keep—'

'You think hiding the truth *protects* me?' Her jaw trembles. 'You think *lying* to me, talking about how *strong* I am while treating me like glass – *that's* protection?'

I shake my head, unable to bear the way she's spun it. 'No. No, I wasn't lying—'

'Yes. You were.' Her voice cracks. 'Because if you believed I was strong – if you really trusted me to hold it together – you wouldn't have hidden this from me. I expect it from Taylor. I can cope with it from Taylor. But *you*...'

'I was scared, Sadie. Scared of what would happen if you knew—'

'If I knew, I'd shatter, right?'

I reach out, trembling, desperate to bridge the distance, to soften the blow – *anything* to stop this. But she jerks back, eyes wild, tears spilling over, each one a knife through my heart.

'You played house with me, pretended like everything was okay—'

'We had the situation in hand. Taylor was okay. Axel was—'

'For fuck's sake, Theo! It doesn't matter how in hand you had it, *I* should have known. He's *my* abuser. *My* ex. And he hurt *my* sister. And instead of telling me, you bring me here under the *pretence* of a *holiday*. Treating me and Lottie to a *dream* vacation. When all the while, you were really just hiding me like some kid who couldn't handle her own reality?'

'No— no, I was trying to protect you. Trying to do what's best for you.'

She lets out a short, bitter laugh. 'There it is, again. Protection. Just like Danny. He was all about protecting me, knowing what was best for me...'

Her words slice deeper than shouting ever could. Danny. Me. The *same*?

'All that stuff you said, all that stuff you had me believing – but you're no better. Making me feel like I'm weak, powerless. Something to fix. To control...' She chokes on the word. 'And you,' she points at me, voice low and lethal, 'you did the exact same thing. Only you smiled while you did it.'

Acid burns the back of my throat. 'No, Sadie—'

'Yes, Theo. Yes!'

'I just wanted to keep you happy—'

'Happy in ignorance? You think that's what I want? My God, Theo, how can you think that's okay? Not to tell me that *my ex* hurt *my sister* trying to get to *me*. There's no justification in the world for that.'

There is. There's one. And it's hammering against my ribs, desperate to break free. Love. I love her.

It hits like a sucker punch as I drown in her gaze. Pain etched in every line of her sweet face – a face I know better than my own. A pain *I* caused.

But how do I say it now? How do I tell her I love her, when in her eyes I'm no better than Danny – the man who twisted love into something so cruel, so poisonous, it drained the life from her?

'I couldn't stand to see him take anything more from you,' I say, the words barely above a whisper. 'I couldn't let him hurt you again.'

'I could've coped with him hurting me again,' she says quietly. 'What I can't cope with is you doing it.'

She shakes her head, then goes still. Behind her tears, the pain falls away. What's left in her heart-wrenching blues is colder. Quieter. Final. Like she sees me clearly now – the whole of me – and doesn't like what she sees.

I want to deny it. Say she's wrong. Say *anything*.

But I can't.

Because she's right.

And it guts me – draining my words, my breath, my body.

'I thought you believed in me, Theo. I thought you saw strength in me – enough to face the past, enough to move on. But all this time, you weren't helping me heal. You were helping me hide. Worse, you told yourself it was the opposite.' She draws a breath and swipes away the tears from her cheeks, lifts her chin. 'I thought Danny broke me. I thought you broke me seven years ago. But it's nothing compared to this. You didn't see me then. And you definitely don't see me now.'

'That's not true, Sadie.' I take a step towards her, hoping proximity might somehow fix what I've shattered, help her to believe what I'm saying. 'I *do* see you.'

'No,' she says, clear and unforgiving. 'You still see Taylor's little sister. And I can live with her seeing me that way. But not *you*. This is over, Theo, whatever *this* was. We're leaving.'

'You can't just go.' I reach for her, both hands out.

She flinches like *I'm* poison. 'Oh, yes I can.'

'But it's not safe,' I say weakly.

'I'd rather take my chances alone than be with someone I don't trust. I don't know who you are any more.'

'You *do*.' The space between us turns glacial, and I stumble forward, the ground falling away beneath me. 'You know me better than anyone else in this world. You *know* you do.'

Something chases over her face, something I want to run after and hold onto, but it's gone too quick to name.

'I thought I did. But the man I knew would've trusted me with the truth – and held me while I came to terms with it. This man... It doesn't matter any more. Because I know now, I don't need you. I don't need Danny. I don't need anyone to hold me up. Goodbye, Theo.'

She spins and strides away.

'Please, Sadie.' I rush after her, panic driving me half-mad as I block her path. 'At least let me drive you.'

'No.' She stiffens, eyes like steel. 'I'll get there on my own – start the way I mean to go on. Just me and Lottie. That was always the plan until you—' She breaks off, eyes dashing away. 'Just let me go.'

'But where will you stay?'

'That's not your concern any more.'

'At least call Taylor, get her—'

'No!' She shoots me a glare so sharp it cuts me in two. 'You've *both* done enough.'

And then she walks.

Not runs.

Walks.

And I let her.

Because this time, she isn't running away an eighteen-year-old girl with her heart crushed; she's walking with her head held high, more certain of who she is and what she wants, and that isn't me.

And I don't blame her.

She's stronger than I ever gave her credit for – fighting for the life she wants, while I clung to fear and called it protection.

Worse, I told myself I was keeping her safe, when really, I was keeping myself safe – from the truth, from the risk, from the weight of loving her out loud.

I'm the coward in this story.

And my greatest weakness was the one thing I should've been strong enough to say all along...

I love you.

18

SADIE

I'm lost.

Not physically.

But mentally. Emotionally. Completely lost.

Walking away from Theo on the path hadn't been fun – but it had been easy. Throwing clothes into cases, making excuses to Isla and Lottie, pasting on a brave face while I got us the hell out of there.

All doable.

Because it kept me busy.

Kept me moving. Kept the emotional tsunami at bay.

But now I'm on the train to London's King's Cross, Lottie tucked into my side – her and Dino quietly absorbed in her tablet – there's nothing left to distract me. Nothing to hold back the thoughts. The heartbreak. The truth crashing over me.

How could he have done this to me?

The one man I thought I could trust. I could let go with. Be real with. Be *me*.

It's soul-destroying. I'm not just mourning what we had – what I *thought* we had – but grieving the future I foolishly let in.

And it's not lost on me, the irony. How I stood there and told him I could do it all on my own, when right now, being alone is the last thing I want.

I think of Taylor. Of Danny getting to her. And it kills me – knowing I brought him to her door.

She *should've* told me, and I'm angry. So angry that she didn't.

But the guilt runs deeper.

I pull out my phone and glance at the series of missed calls, all Taylor, and messages:

> **TAYLOR**
>
> Call me, please. I'm so sorry xx

I believe her. I do. I just wish it didn't hurt so much.

> **UNKNOWN NUMBER**
>
> My men will meet you at the station and take you wherever you want to go. Axel

My teeth grind. Taylor or Theo – one of them has been on to Axel.

But I'd be lying if I said there wasn't a part of me that felt relief. Because being angry at Theo kept me from fully thinking about Danny. And the thought of coming face to face with him – Lottie in tow – knowing the rage it must've taken to drive him this far...

It's a showdown I'm in no shape to face.

My phone buzzes as I'm staring at it, and my heart flips over:

> **THEO**
>
> I know you hate me, but please believe me when I say I'm sorry. More than words can ever say. T xx

Hate *you*? I wish I could hate you!

That's why it hurts so goddamn much. It's not Taylor, it's *you*.

Because I was the idiot who fell in love with him all over again. I was the idiot who thought he could possibly see me and love me back. I was the idiot who'd started to hope for a future as perfect as those families on the beach. As perfect as *us* on the beach.

My fingers tremble as I lift the phone and take in the photo on the home screen. It's Lottie eating ice cream – the laughter in her eyes, the hands holding her by the waist... Theo.

I press my fist to my mouth, smothering the rising sob. *Oh, God, Theo.*

And then I do the only thing I know I can: I call the one person I know will catch me.

It picks up on the first ring...

'Sadie! Thank God!'

'Tay,' I croak out. 'I need you.'

* * *

Theo

The house is cold and quiet, and I can't bear it.

Not the silence.

Not Isla's concerned gaze.

Not my conscience.

And definitely not my imagination that's running wild with thoughts of Danny getting to her.

So I do the only thing I can: I get in the car and drive to London.

It's the longest journey of my life.

And when I get there, I'm met with the very thing I was trying to outrun.

Emptiness.

Only here, it's worse.

In Pembrokeshire, all trace of them was gone.

Here, in my apartment, they're everywhere I look.

Lottie's shoes scattered by the door. Her boxes of toys lined up against the wall. Colouring pencils still spread across the kitchen table. Her books. Her cups. Her joy.

And Sadie—

I can smell her in the air. That faint trace of perfume I'd know anywhere. *Just like Danny...*

I clench my fists, grind my teeth. No, not like Danny. *Never* like Danny.

My phone buzzes and I snatch it up. Hope against hope that it's Sadie.

It's not.

AXEL

They've taken her to Taylor's. She's good. Meet me at Royal HQ.

Good? She's not fucking good. Because I broke her. Me. Not Danny. *Me.*

ME

I'm not fit for company.

AXEL

I'm not asking. 9pm. Else, I'm coming to you.

ME

I don't want to talk.

AXEL

Who said anything about talking, I plan on drinking…

* * *

Sadie

'Did she go down okay?' Taylor asks, pressing a glass of wine into my hand.

'Yeah, she's exhausted. A morning with Isla's grandkids, then several train journeys, and…'

'Isla?'

'Theo's housekeeper. She took her to—'

The lump in my throat swells, and I cover my mouth to stop the tears from falling.

'Come on, darling. Let's get you sat down.'

She gently steers me into the living room. The space is just as impressive and minimalist as Theo's, but hers feels softer – all creams and pale woods, perfectly Taylor chic. And here I am, the undone mess right in the centre of it all. Like always.

But I'm too hurt to care.

I fold myself into the sofa, curling my legs beneath me, and take a slow sip of wine. I don't taste a drop. Every sense is caught in my thoughts – on Lottie, how happy she'd been coming back with Isla, how her joy softened into sadness when I told her we were leaving. Leaving without Theo.

'She's going to miss him so much, Tay. And I don't know how I'm going to explain it to her.'

Taylor studies me intently. 'Are you sure it's her you're worried about?'

My heart stutters, my eyes clashing with hers. 'Of course it is, I let her get attached and now...'

'Now what? You're acting like you're never going to see him again.'

'I don't *want* to see him again.'

'I don't think that's true.'

'He hurt me, Tay. You both did. I had a right to know. You should've trusted me with it.'

Her face crumbles. 'I know, darling, I know, and I'm so sorry. But that night, you were a changed woman. When I thought about how you were at the airport, I just couldn't bear you taking a backwards step. That man hurt you enough.'

'It has nothing on the pain of being lied to by Theo.'

'He didn't lie to you, honey. He just didn't tell you what happened because I told him not to. I wanted to protect—'

'Don't you start with the protection thing. I'm not a kid any more.'

'No, I know you're not.' She strokes my hair back from my face, her eyes welling up. 'And I... I think you're in love with him, aren't you?'

'What?' I choke out. How can she know? 'What did he say?'

'It's what neither of you are saying. I can see it in you. I think I saw it in you that night, but I told myself it was just the joy of seeing you happy again.'

'I'm not... I don't...' The lie dies on my lips. 'Oh Tay, I'm such an idiot. I loved him back then, you know. Before college. Before Danny. And he knew it. I told him. But he couldn't see me as anything more than your little sister – he still can't.'

'Are you sure about that?'

Sure?

I break down, head shaking. She pulls me in, holds me tight, gently shushing as the tears finally come – tears I haven't let fall since I walked away from Theo.

I'm not sure about anything any more. All that rubbish I fed him about standing on my own, knowing my own mind. Who's the liar now?

But I have to be sure. I have to be strong. For Lottie. For me.

I've got a new life to start.

Just... not tonight.

Tonight, I can cry.

Tomorrow, I'll stand tall and move forward with my daughter.

Just like I always meant to...

Before I fell in love with him all over again.

* * *

Theo

I'm on my third drink when Axel levels me with *that* stare.

'You said we weren't going to talk.'

'I lied.'

I drop my head into my hands, jaw clenched tight against the churn in my gut.

'Not talking about it doesn't make it disappear,' he says quietly.

'And what would you know about it?' I snap, flicking my head up. 'You never loved anyone in your life.'

He doesn't even flinch. But I do.

'I'm sorry, Ax. I shouldn't have said that.'

There's something in his eye that I can't read, something that gives me a moment's pause. It's not quite pain. It's something else. Like he's holding back on me.

'Ax—'

'I know enough to know what this is,' he says over me. 'Did you tell her?'

'Tell her what?'

'What do you mean, "what"? Did you tell her you're in love with her?'

I shake my head. 'How could I, after all that?'

A ghost of a smile tugs at the corner of his mouth. 'Well at least you're not denying it any more.'

He's right. I'm not. Because I can't.

It's in every breath I take and will be until my last.

'So let me get this straight: she left you because you were keeping secrets from her?'

'Yeah.'

'And yet, you're still keeping the biggest secret of all to yourself.'

'It's not that simple.'

'No?'

'The last thing she wants to hear from me is that I love her.'

'How can you know that?'

'Because it's exactly what Danny did to her. Every time he hurt her, he'd say it was because he loved her. That he was protecting her, keeping her safe from herself.' The words rise like bile in my throat. 'I was no better.'

'You can't seriously be comparing yourself to him?'

'She did. She made that very clear.'

'She was hurting, Theo.'

He rarely uses my forename, and hearing it now makes every word land like a punch.

'Because of *me*.'

'And don't you think it hurt more, because, deep down, she's in love with you too?'

I hold his stare. Something kicks in my chest and I shut it down hard. 'If she did, she certainly doesn't now.'

He leans back, lets out a low, bitter laugh. 'And I'm the one who doesn't know about love?'

'What the fuck's that supposed to mean?'

'Love doesn't give a damn about logic. It digs in and it stays – to hell with what makes sense, what's right, what's fair.'

He hooks his fingers together in his lap, dark eyes staring me down.

'If she loved you before, she'll love you still. You might not feel worthy of it right now, but I'm telling you, she could do no better than you. And you owe her the truth. Hell, you owe it to yourself to tell her. Then I'll let you drown your sorrows in peace. But until then...'

'And what if she doesn't want to hear it?'

'At least you will have told her your truth, and the choice will be hers to make.'

I knock my whisky back. Let it scorch the hope clawing at my throat.

'Since when have you not gone after what you want, Tanner?'

Since the day I fell in love with a woman I thought I could never have...

19

SADIE

I sit in the sleek, sunlit office of Empowered Publishing, palms damp, heart thudding like I've smuggled a secret into the building. Which I suppose I have. Me.

Dressed in a pale-blue, linen shift dress and white trainers – my busy-mum version of boardroom chic. Taylor was horrified when she saw me ('You're meeting a publisher, not doing the school run!'), but even she had to admit, with an OTT sigh, that it was 'very you'.

As for Lucile Baldwin, she's exactly how I imagined her – composed, warm, quietly fierce. Bobbed, blonde hair. Piercing, blue eyes. Mid-fifties. She's already walked me through their vision: how they see the blog evolving, how the book could push my reach even further. She talks like I'm some movement leader when all I did was write. Write and survive.

'I hope we've made it clear,' she says gently, 'that your story is safe with us. *You* are safe with us. And we believe in what you're doing.'

My throat tightens. Not because of her words, but because I've heard similar before – from someone else. Someone who looked at me like I was worth every good thing.

It's been three days since I last saw Theo, and not a single hour's passed without his face breaking through. Or the memory of what I said. What I accused him of.

Just like Danny.

'Sadie?'

I snap back into the room. Lucile's watching me closely, brows knitted in concern.

'Sorry,' I murmur, becoming aware of my fists clenched tight upon the desk. I smooth them out, place my palms against the cool, glass surface. 'You were saying?'

'There are ways we can publish anonymously, if that's what feels right. But like I mentioned in my email, if you did want to go public, we'd support you completely. Full press, media training, PR... extra security if you feel you need it.' Her eyes flick to Mike – my close protection detail courtesy of Axel, stationed in the main office behind us, just visible through the glass. 'You'd control every step. The message, the moment.'

I nod slowly, my pulse picking up.

'Sometimes,' she adds, 'stepping into the light changes everything. It makes the story more real. It shows people that the woman behind the words isn't just a survivor, but someone who took her voice back. And maybe inspires others to do the same.'

I close my eyes, take a breath, and I see it.

Me, standing in front of a room. Face no longer hidden. Speaking up. I feel fear, sure. Nerves, too. It's been so long since I've shown myself. Longer still without the fear of ridicule. But beneath it all, I feel something else. Power. Possibility. Pride.

And one name rises to the surface: Theo.

Because he was the first to believe I could do this. Even when he faltered, it wasn't doubt – it was fear *for* me. He wasn't trying to silence me. He was trying to shield me from someone else's venom.

And wouldn't I do the same for him? Stand between him and anyone who'd try to hurt him? God, yes. In a heartbeat.

He's not Danny.

He's *nothing* like Danny.

But I let my pain speak for me. And I let him think I believed the worst.

Because in reality, I *was* terrified. Not of Danny, but of him. Terrified that he was going to break my heart again.

I ended it, not because of what he did. I ended it because ultimately, it meant leaving on my terms. Staying in control. And then I wielded that control like a weapon, hurting Theo in the process. *Now who's like Danny...*

My breath escapes me in a rush.

'Sadie?' Lucile prompts softly.

'Yes.' I nod swiftly. 'Let's do it. Let's go public.'

Her perfectly made-up lips stretch into a smile. 'Excellent. Let's get into the details.'

'Actually...' I'm already rising. 'Would you mind if we did this another day? There's somewhere I need to be.'

Because I can't bear another second of him thinking the worst – thinking *he's* the worst – because of *me*.

I owe him the truth, my *full* truth. Even if it means reliving the heartbreak I've been trying to run from the moment I crashed back into his life with my daughter in tow.

He may not want my love, but there's no escaping it.

My heart was always meant for him.

Minutes later, I flee the fancy tower block, heart racing, feet pounding. Mike gestures to the blacked-out Range Rover pulling up, and I make a beeline for it.

But the moment it stops, the rear door swings open – *huh?*

A figure steps out...

Dark-blond hair, mussed like it's been manhandled for days.

Tall, broad frame. White tee. Faded jeans. That easy slouch I'd know in my sleep.

My feet falter. My heart too.

Theo.

He straightens fully, his ravaged green gaze capturing mine and stealing the last of my breath. The ache of everything unsaid barrels through me all at once.

'Theo?' I whisper, the name torn straight from my chest.

'Sadie,' he breathes, as if it almost breaks him. 'Please don't be mad at Axel for telling me where you were. I had to see you. I didn't want to do this at Taylor's – not with Lottie there – and this felt like the only chance to—'

'You don't need to explain,' I cut in, my heart lurching at his guilt when it should be me suffering it. Not him. Never him.

Tears spill faster than I can stop them.

I take a step closer, then another. 'I was coming to find you.'

His eyes widen into mine. He's so close now, I can feel the warmth radiating off his body, catch his familiar scent curling through the air. The desperation to lean in, to touch him, to breathe him in fully, is like nothing I've ever known.

'You were?'

'There's so much I need to say to you—'

A horn blares across the street. People bustle past. Mike stands a discreet distance away but hears every word. It all presses in on a moment I don't want us to share.

I swipe away the tears and ask, 'Would you take a drive with me?'

He doesn't hesitate. Just pulls the door open wider...

'Home, Miss Stone?' the driver asks as I slip inside, and Mike takes the front seat.

I glance at Theo as he gets in beside me.

'Please, but would you mind taking the long way?'

'No problem.'

The privacy glass slides up, sealing us into a quiet, humming stillness.

I clasp my hands in my lap and turn—

'Sade,' he says.

'Theo,' I say at the same time.

We smile. The smallest of gestures. The biggest of aches.

'Please let me go first,' I say quietly. 'Because I owe you an apology...'

His eyes rake over my face, searching, trying to understand.

'I hate that it's taken me this long to see through the pain to all that I did wrong.'

'You didn't—'

'I did.' I hold his gaze, a single tear escaping. 'Don't tell me I didn't, Theo. I *did*.' I take a shaky breath. 'Even saying your name in the same breath as Danny's was wrong. You're nothing like him. You never were. I was scared, and I lashed out. I said the one thing I knew would push you away. Because I was afraid. Not of you hurting me...' I swallow '...but of loving you again.'

His eyes flash, his mouth parting to speak, but I throw up a hand to stop him.

'Please. I need to get this out. All of it. What you and Taylor did... it gave me the excuse I needed to end it. To run. And I'm sorry. So, so sorry. You believed in me, even when I didn't,' I whisper. 'Even when you kept Danny from me, it wasn't because you doubted me. It was because you were scared for me. And I wasn't honest with you.'

I take his hand, needing to hold onto him as I say, 'I know you didn't want to hear this seven years ago, and maybe you still don't. But I can't keep it in.'

I wet my lips, take one last steadying breath.

'I'm in love with you, Theo. My heart belongs to you. It always has. Whether you want it or not, I—'

He surges forward before I can finish, both hands diving into my hair as his mouth slams into mine. Hard. Desperate. Like he's terrified I'll disappear if he waits another second.

And I feel it too. The hunger, the ache, the need that's lived beneath my skin for far too long. I whimper against him, taking his all, giving my all. No fear. Just this. My love for him.

When he finally pulls back, we're gasping, breaths mingling, foreheads pressed together as his hands cradle my face.

'That wasn't quite the reaction I expected,' I say, breathless.

He lets out a hoarse, broken laugh. 'You just handed me my every dream in one breath.'

'It was definitely more of a speech...' I laugh softly, my voice trembling. 'But your every dream?'

He leans back just enough to take me in, that reverent look in his eye – the one I've come to adore.

'I love you, Sadie Stone. I loved you seven years, and I wouldn't let myself have you. I'm not making that mistake again. I love you, and I want you. And I'm sorry if you can't handle my protection, because I will guard you and Lottie with everything I have and everything I am. Nothing and no one gets to hurt you again.'

'You want to be our knight in shining armour?' I tease through the tears.

'I'll be whatever you and Lottie need me to be,' he says without hesitation. Then he kisses my forehead, my cheek, my lips. 'Seven years of loving you, of knowing you were out there and not mine, I don't want to spend another without you. You and Lottie – you're my world now.'

I shake my head, joy swelling in my chest. 'I can't believe this is really happening.'

'You better bloody believe it,' he murmurs, kissing me again. This one slower, more thorough – a claiming and a homecoming.

I melt into him, into the warmth of everything I thought I'd lost.

And for the first time in years – maybe ever – I let myself believe in happy endings.

The car slows. Mike's voice crackles through the speaker. 'We're here. Want us to circle the block again?'

Theo breaks away to say, 'What do you think?'

'There's a girl I know who's been desperate to see you…'

He smiles. 'She and me, both.'

I smile with him. 'We're good to get out, thanks, Mike.'

We step into the lift of Taylor's building, hearts still thundering, bodies close but nerves high. When the doors open onto my sister's penthouse, I can already hear Lottie's laughter.

We follow it to find Taylor sprawled on the floor in top-to-toe Chanel, hair piled on top of her head in a way I've *never* seen it before, helping Lottie build what appears to be an elaborate cardboard city. There are juice cartons. There's glitter. Tiaras and stray plushies. It's chaos. But it's happy chaos.

Taylor looks up, startled. 'Oh! Hey— How did it—?' She freezes mid-sentence, eyes landing on Theo. On our hands.

Lottie turns, her face lighting up. 'Uncle Feo!' she shrieks, abandoning the glittery mess and launching herself at him. 'I knew Mummy would find you!'

Theo catches her midair, hugging her tight to his chest, his eyes closing like the moment is too much to hold in.

'She found me,' he whispers.

'Well,' Taylor breathes, brushing off her Chanel as she gets to her feet. 'Look who finally pulled their heads out of their arses.' She crosses her arms and zeroes in on Theo. 'Just so we're clear, I'm thrilled you two have figured things out. Love, healing, happily ever after – big yay. But we're still going to have words. Because when I said, "watch out for my sister," I didn't mean with your penis.'

Theo chokes as I groan.

'Tay,' I say, 'there are little ears about.'

Taylor shrugs, all faux innocence. 'Just stating facts. And I'm happy for you. I'm also legally obligated to make him sweat a little. Now go make out or whatever. I'll be in the kitchen opening wine and *not* thinking about any of this.' She turns on her heel, tossing over her shoulder, 'Though, Theo, you hurt her, there won't be a third-act reconciliation. There'll be a shovel.'

He watches her go, wide-eyed, and I smother a laugh.

'Now you know how I felt growing up. It's a bit different when she's related to you, hey?' I say. 'Welcome to the family.'

'Are we a weal family now?' Lottie says, eyes darting between us, her tiny index finger pointing. 'Mummy. Daddy. Me.'

My heart stumbles as I meet Theo's gaze.

'The realest,' he says.

And I know, deep in my bones, it's true.

No more running. No more fear.

Just us. Just love. A family and a home.

20

SADIE

Four Weeks Later...

The lights are hot, the crowd louder than I expected, but I'm standing.

Not hiding.

I grip the edges of the lectern, fingers steady, pulse calmer than I thought possible. My name flashes on the purple screen behind me. Bold white letters. *SADIE STONE*. Not *Anon*. Not a ghost.

I wear a lavender dress, its simple design all me, its quiet elegance perfect for today. Gentle yet resolute – a beacon of hope, as the PR team likes to say. My make-up is soft and natural, my hair smooth and loose around my shoulders. No unnecessary embellishments.

Just me.

The auditorium is packed – publishers, journalists, survivors, allies. People who read the blog and whispered, 'Me too,' in the dark. But scattered among the strangers are the faces that matter most.

Theo and Taylor, front row, beaming up at me. Rachael and Charlene too, eyes shining with tears and admiration.

Axel, arms crossed and watchful, two of his security team posted discreetly at the back.

Lucile, seated beside a small panel of speakers, nodding at me with quiet encouragement.

And I know Lottie isn't far away. Theo's mum is taking her to the park for a special outing because though my daughter will one day learn of this, now is not the time or the place. She's finally getting to be a child again, and I will cherish every day our freedom brings her.

I breathe it all in slowly, then...

'My name is Mercedes Stone. Sadie Stone to those who know me well or knew of me before I went into hiding. For the past two years, I've been writing anonymously about surviving domestic abuse. I shared my story in pieces because that's how I lived it: in fragments. Scattered between shame, silence, and the slow reclaiming of myself.'

A hush falls over the room.

'But today, I'm not hiding any more.'

The room explodes in applause, but I barely hear it.

I feel it. In my bones. In my spine.

'I'm here because no one should have to feel powerless in their own life. I'm here because truth is louder than fear. Because healing doesn't happen in the dark.'

When I finish, they stand. Every single person.

Cameras flash. People wipe tears. Lucile moves to the stage with a wide smile. The panel begins, questions are asked, and I answer them all. No shame. No stuttering. Just honesty.

I feel Theo's gaze on me the whole time, a tether I don't necessarily need, but most definitely want.

When the event starts to wind down, people begin to disperse. Handshakes, hugs, compliments. I'm basking in pride when I catch movement from the corner of my eye.

And my blood runs cold.

Danny.

He's leaning against the far wall like he belongs here. Like this is his story. Dark eyes lock onto mine, then that slow, knowing smile curves at his lips, like he's already two steps ahead.

I freeze. For a second.

Then I step towards him.

His smirk falters.

'I guess all it took was a stage,' he sneers, keeping his voice low. 'You finally learned how to beg for attention like the rest of them.'

I stop two feet from him. I don't shake. I don't cry.

I burn.

'I'm not begging,' I say, voice razor-sharp. 'I'm owning what you tried to destroy.'

He scoffs. 'This little circus won't last. You think these people will care when the buzz dies? You think he,' his eyes flick past me – right at Theo, 'will still want you when you're not the poster girl for trauma?'

I don't flinch.

'You don't get to talk about him,' I say. 'And you don't get to talk to me. Not any more.'

'I made you who you are,' he hisses. 'Everything you are is because of me.'

'No.' I step closer. 'Everything I am is in spite of you.'

He starts to reach for me – some pathetic, knee-jerk grab for control – but then two large shadows step in. Axel's men. Each grabs an arm, locking him down.

'Danny Jones, you're in violation of your restraining order. You're coming with us.'

Danny jerks, tries to twist free, but it's useless. His eyes find mine one last time, spitting fury. But I don't return it.

I just watch.

Watch him be removed from my space, my moment, my life.

A second later, I feel a presence behind me. No words, just his soft breath.

Theo.

I turn.

He's standing there like he was that day in the park when I first broke down in front of him. Not asking anything of me. Just there. Solid. Real.

'I saw the whole thing,' he says quietly.

'Good,' I reply. My voice is steady, but my heart is a riot. 'Because I want you to see who I am now. Not just who I am when I'm with you, but who I am in here.'

I press my hand to my chest and his eyes don't leave mine.

'I do.'

* * *

Theo

I do.

Two words, but they don't even scratch the surface.

Because what I see standing in front of me isn't just the woman I love. It's a force of nature. Sadie Stone – the woman who once broke down on me in a park, who flinched when the world got too loud, who tucked her light into corners just to survive – is standing in the sun now.

Unapologetic. Unshaken. Unstoppable.

And I've never loved anyone more in my life.

The crowd fades. The room fades. Everything fades, except her.

'I wanted to run to you when he showed up,' I say softly, stepping closer, 'but you didn't need me.'

'No,' she says just as soft. 'But I wanted you here.'

That undoes me.

'I've never been prouder,' I say, and I don't care that my voice cracks. 'I've seen how you wrote your way out of the dark. How you fought your way back into the light. And now you're standing in front of the whole damn world and showing them what healing looks like.' I laugh under my breath, brushing a stray blonde wisp from her cheek. 'I think I fell in love with you all over again today.'

She blinks rapidly, eyes shimmering with both tears and pride, and wraps her arms around my waist like it's the only place she wants to be.

'I didn't just do this for me,' she whispers. 'I did it for all those people like me. I did it for Lottie. And I did it for us.'

Us.

God, I never thought I'd hear that word again. Not with her.

But now it feels like it's carved into stone. Unbreakable. Like her.

'I love you, Theo.'

'I love you too,' I say, pulling her in and kissing her deep.

It's not desperate. Not frantic or pained or laced with fear. It's sure. Solid. Full.

The world keeps spinning, cameras flashing, people chattering... but in this moment, it's only us.

'*Ew!*'

Or not. We both freeze, pulling apart just enough to see a familiar little face scrunched in theatrical horror at knee height.

'Lottie,' Sadie breathes, half-laughing, half-mortified.

'Granny Anna, we need soap. Or a hose.'

'We do?' my mum says, looking puzzled. 'Sorry, she was desperate to come and see what the fuss was about, and we figured you were pretty much done.'

'What's this about needing a hose?' Taylor says, coming up behind them.

'It's a long story,' Sadie says, laughing.

Taylor raises an eyebrow. 'I think I'm going to need champagne for this. Bar, everyone?'

'Don't need to ask me twice,' my mother says as we all pile out.

Sadie signals to her friends over the crowd to join us and I lean down to murmur in her ear, 'I love you.'

She turns into me. 'Always and forever.'

'But we're never buying a hose.'

'Hell, no.'

* * *

MORE FROM RACHAEL STEWART

Another book from Rachael Stewart, *Filthy Rich Redemption*, is available to order now here:

https://mybook.to/FilthyRedemptionBackAd

ACKNOWLEDGEMENTS

To the incredible team at Boldwood – thank you for everything you do behind the scenes. From the brilliant editors who helped shape this story into its best self, to the marketing magicians, audio wizards, packaging pros, cover designers and so on – your talent and enthusiasm have made launching this new series a true joy. I'm so excited for what's to come, and that's in no small part thanks to you.

A special and heartfelt thank you to my fabulous editor, Megan Haslam. Thank you for welcoming me into the Boldwood family and for believing in my stories as much as I do. This series wouldn't exist without you!

To my nephew, Parker, whose giggly, wild ways brought Lottie to life – thank you, you little monkey! And to your parents, Mike and Rach – thank you for letting me borrow his mischief-making spirit for this book. It's funny how quickly you forget the chaos of your own kids in the terror-toddler stage! Having him stay is equal parts exhausting and exhilarating, and I wouldn't change a second of it. Love you to the moon and back!

Thank you, as ever, to you my amazing readers. For picking up my stories, reading, reviewing, and sharing your love with the world. While I write from the heart for myself, it's *your* joy, laughter, and messages that make this journey so rewarding. I truly hope this series gives you everything you hope for in a romance – I can't wait to hear what you think!

Last, but never least – to my kids and my wonderful husband. Thank you for giving me the time and space to lose myself in my characters and their world. I couldn't do this without your support. I love you all so very much xxx

ABOUT THE AUTHOR

Rachael Stewart is a bestselling romance author, writing billionaire romance for Boldwood.

Sign up to Rachael Stewart's mailing list for news, competitions and updates on future books.

Visit Rachael's website: www.rachaelstewartauthor.com

Follow Rachael on social media here:

- facebook.com/rachaelstewartauthor
- x.com/rach_b52
- instagram.com/rachaelstewart3
- tiktok.com/@rachaelstewartauthor
- bookbub.com/authors/rachael-stewart

ALSO BY RACHAEL STEWART

The Karma Club Series

The Payback Plan by Amy Andrews

How to Get Even by Pippa Roscoe

The Puck Stops Here by Rachael Stewart

Settling the Score by Clare Connelly

Filthy Rich Billionaires

Filthy Rich Temptation

Filthy Rich Redemption

Filthy Rich Seduction

EVER AFTER

xᴏxᴏ

JOIN BOLDWOOD'S **ROMANCE COMMUNITY** FOR SWEET AND SPICY BOOK RECS WITH ALL YOUR FAVOURITE TROPES!

SIGN UP TO OUR
NEWSLETTER

HTTPS://BIT.LY/BOLDWOODEVERAFTER

Boldwood

Boldwood Books is an award-winning fiction publishing company seeking out the best stories from around the world.

Find out more at www.boldwoodbooks.com

Join our reader community for brilliant books, competitions and offers!

Follow us
@BoldwoodBooks
@TheBoldBookClub

Sign up to our weekly deals newsletter

https://bit.ly/BoldwoodBNewsletter